BLUE LILIES

NIGHTGARDEN SAGA #6

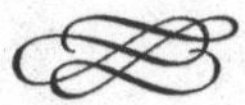

LUCY HOLDEN

FEHU PRESS

For my mother, Bev, who is dancing somewhere.

There is also a prequel, told from Antoine's perspective, available on my website. Go to www.paulaconstant.com to download.

PROLOGUE

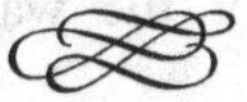

Dear Tessa,

Fall came and went, then winter. Now the first shoots of spring are poking through the earth. I feel as if the time has passed in a haze. In just a few weeks, Antoine and I will meet our twins in person. It still doesn't feel real. Sometimes I stand in front of the mirror staring at my belly, thinking of everything that led me to here. But reality isn't like that, is it? We don't carry all that has gone before with us, into every new day. We can only live one day, one moment, one experience, at a time. So no matter all that has gone before, when I look at my belly now, all I know is that I'm pregnant with twin girls I can't wait to meet. That I'm in love with my husband more than I ever imagined possible. And that my world feels full of love, and hope.

I do try to remind myself of the other side of that reality. That my twin girls are time travelers, for example, with powers none of us understand yet. Or the fact that my husband is a vampire. That Keziah, an ancient and dangerous enemy, is lurking unseen somewhere in our world, lying in wait for the birth of our twins so she can take them for her own. Or that the only way I can be sure to keep myself and our girls safe from Keziah is to become a vampire myself, the moment after they are born.

My sensible mind knows all those things. Somehow, though, pregnancy has put a marshmallow wall between my sensible mind and the world of my heart. I spend pretty much all my time on the heart side of the wall, blissfully ignoring the sensible arguments.

When I do allow myself to think of the time after the twins are born, I want to seize every day that I have left in my human body. That isn't hard. Being pregnant with twins is more than enough to keep me firmly focused on my physical body. I am so huge Antoine insists on carrying me down the stairs every time he catches me trying to take them on foot, and weeding my garden is a long-distant memory. I can barely see my feet, let alone what is growing underneath them. At this point, the thought of having an unchanging body that doesn't feel pain is like a fantasy. So I guess you could say that while I'm definitely focused on my human body, right now I'm not feeling any sadness at all about trading it in for a more resilient model.

I can only make jokes like that in these letters to you, since everyone else seems to find them upsetting. Antoine evades any real discussion about my becoming a vampire. We're in agreement it has to happen. But I know that even if he understands it is the smartest course, part of him hates the thought of what I may become.

I don't believe the magic that runs through my veins will become a dark force, as Caleb's did. Antoine's blood, and the medicine woman's spirit held within it, activated the natural magic in mine in a way Caleb's never was. If we are right, Keziah killed Caleb before he was fully activated. Nor was he an Abatey, the living embodiment of a water spirit. But even if I feel certain I will not become what Caleb was, I'd be lying if I said I'm not afraid of what will happen. The truth is that nobody really knows what I will be after I become a vampire.

There is a lot we don't know.

Tate and Iara went away soon after our wedding. Iara isn't safe here, and Tate wanted her help to discover what he can about Taíno and Warao history. At least, that's what he told us. By the way he was looking at Iara when they left, I suspect there's more to him wanting her by his side than he is admitting, even to himself.

Tate thinks the local stories in Haiti and down in Venezuela might tell us more about Keziah. The wolves, too, have their own legends, so Remy and Connor are working together to find what they can. Since the arrival of Guidry, Antoine's old friend and Remy's distant ancestor, all trace of animosity between them seems gone. The knowledge Guidry brought—that Antoine's blood not only made them wolf but also imparted the gift of immortality—has been both liberating and, I suspect, daunting. While the knowledge seems to have set Connor free, allowing him to finally see a true future with Cass, I suspect it has thrown up new challenges for the pack.

Despite the shock of adjusting to an eternity as a wolf, Remy remains devoted to Avery, who is away at college. Remy's sudden willingness to help research Keziah is due more, I think, to a desire to remain linked to Avery than anything else. By the way Remy looks every time Avery's name is mentioned, and the amount of time he spends talking to her on the phone, distance isn't a barrier to their rekindled relationship.

Callie has already been accepted into Old Miss to study pre-med. I'm going to miss her terribly when she goes away to college. By then, the twins will have been born.

And that brings me back to where I started.

The reality, both in my heart and my mind, is that I can't even begin to imagine what life will look like after our girls are born. I don't know what I will be, or even what, exactly, they will be. I try to think of everything you told me, Tessa. That the twins visited you all your life. That you saw them grown into young women. That they helped bring my wedding dress to life. I tell myself that all those things mean I have nothing to worry about.

But another, fearful part of me wonders if all those memories belong to one of the water paths Iara spoke about. If something happens to harm the twins, during the birth or after, will I simply find myself on another water path? Will it be as if they never existed at all? Worst of all, will I be the only one able to remember everything that's happened?

As fantastic as they might seem, these are the thoughts that haunt me and can send me spiraling into terror.

The water lilies that showed just above the water when I first discovered my pregnancy are yet to unfurl. Over winter the color of the buds changed, the petals beneath now showing a deep indigo. They look more like an Egyptian lotus than they do a lily. I've never seen their like grow here. To be honest, I'm not certain I've ever seen anything like them.

But they have yet to flower, Tessa. They should have unfurled long ago, and yet they remain tightly closed, barely showing above the surface of the pond. I check them every morning to make sure they are still there. And every day when I find them still alive, I realize I've been holding my breath, terrified that I will find that they've simply disappeared.

I know this is a long letter. I've been writing to you much more often since the wedding. I guess I know, now, that you're truly here with us. I don't have to wonder if you're listening. I know you are. Every bird call, every whisper of breeze, carries part of you on it. I may no longer be able to touch you, Tessa, or ever see you again. But I know you're with me, and that is the greatest comfort I have.

Outside the air is hushed. Spring might be here, but our garden is still, and waiting, as we all are.

Inside, the twins are moving restlessly.

It won't be long, now, until all our questions are answered . . . one way or another.

Your twin,

Harper

CHAPTER 1

DAWN

It's early morning, and a slow mist rises over the river. I'm sitting with my bare feet in the cool water of the pond in my night garden, staring at the unopened water lilies, as if I can will them to unfurl simply by looking at them. The garden around me is silent and still. Moisture dripping from the trees is the only sound in the dawn hush. I woke an hour ago, when it was still dark, to find Antoine gone. He's been hunting more often than he used to. Although he hasn't said so, I'm certain he's building his strength ahead of the twins' birth. We both know that he's going to need it.

I try to lift my feet out of the water and stand up, but I'm so big now that even the simplest of movements is like a comedy of errors. Finally, I roll over onto my hands and knees, only to find myself staring at a pair of very long, denim-clad legs.

"Can I help at all?" The humor in Antoine's voice is unmistakable. He's standing with his hands thrust into the back pockets of his jeans, his shirt open at the neck and his hair still wet from the shower. He looks like he could have stepped off the cover of a magazine, but his face seems to wear a perpetual frown lately, and even well-fed and rested, he looks

7

drawn, unlike his usual self. We're both scared of what is coming, just as much as we're excited to finally meet our daughters.

"I feel like you're enjoying this just a little too much," I grumble. He gathers me up as easily as if I were a child, rather than the size of a baby elephant, and sets me gently on my feet, his hands still resting loosely on what used to be my hips. He's smiling, the early morning sun picking out the gold in his eyes from the fathomless cobalt behind them, skin glowing bronze. He's impossibly beautiful, and impossible not to love.

"There are a thousand inappropriate jokes I could make about you being on your knees, but by the look on your face, I'm guessing none of them would be wise just now." His voice is low and rich and still makes my stomach turn over.

"Excellent guess."

"Tate called." Antoine picks a leaf out of my hair. "He and Iara are coming back. They should be here in the next few days."

"Good?" I don't know if it is or not. Keziah can sense Iara's presence, just as she can Cass's and Antoine's. The statue Tessa gave me for Iara seems to be a kind of shield, even though Iara can still hear Keziah calling her. We had wondered, when Tate and Iara went to South America, if Keziah would know. We never found out. Keziah disappeared after Cass told her we had bound Iara in the cellar beneath the mansion. Iara remained out of sight after that, until she and Tate went away. Whether Keziah believed Cass or not is a mystery. I doubt she's been wasting the months of my pregnancy, though. Keziah will be back. It's only a question of when.

"Tate said he and Iara are bringing someone back here with them. He wanted to warn me, given how close we are to the twins being born." Antoine seems calm enough. "It's a shaman from Iara's tribe. He offered to come, apparently. Tate thinks he can help protect you during the birth."

"That's a good thing?" Again, I'm not sure.

"I guess so." Antoine looks as unconvinced as I feel. "We'll find out when we meet him."

"A shaman." I say it doubtfully. Sometimes I feel as if we're magnets, drawing every kind of supernatural to us. Equally, if it can help keep our babies safe, I will take any kind of supernatural there is. "We'll have a full house, soon enough. Callie mentioned Jeremiah was talking about coming back for spring break, too."

Since Jeremiah went away to college last fall, the riverside house he and Antoine had once shared has been more or less closed up. Antoine keeps some things there, more so that Jeremiah will know he has a home of his own than for any other reason, I suspect. At Christmas, though, Jeremiah had come straight to the mansion and stayed for the duration. I expect he'll do the same this time. He likes to be close to Antoine, and my due date is right on top of spring break.

"It will be good to see him." Antoine gives me a smile that doesn't quite relax the tension in his eyes. "I'm sure it will be fine." It's not clear if he's talking about the Warao shaman, the full house we'll have, the birth, or my becoming a vampire.

Take your pick. I return his smile with one I'm sure he finds just as unconvincing as I do his. "Of course it will."

His eyes move from my face to the pond behind me, and his smile fades, taking with it the gold from his eyes. "Please tell me you weren't sitting with your feet in that pond."

"I'm not going to suddenly time travel every time I'm in water, Antoine. It would make showering difficult, don't you think?"

"That pond isn't just any water, and you know it." He's unamused by my attempt at levity. "Everything about your garden is filled with magic. It also just happens to be the place Keziah found you last time." His eyes lock onto mine, and although his voice is gentle, all trace of humor is gone. "I think it's time we started being very careful, Harper. We're less than two weeks away from your due date. Keziah will know that as well as we do. She won't be far away."

Despite the mild temperature, I can't suppress a shiver. "Surely we would know if she had come back? The wolves always know if she's nearby. Guidry said there are others of your kind who can help us, if we call on them." Guidry originally came from the same bayous as Remy's pack, though he predates the existing wolves by more than two centuries.

"Yes, we have the alliance with Guidry and the pack. And he assures me the European vampires he knows have offered their help, although I'm reluctant to involve any more supernatural beings than we have already, so I don't intend to take them up on the offer. But even if I did, all the reinforcements in the world can't protect us against Keziah if she finds a way of getting to you or the twins, Harper. We can't let that happen."

"I know." I put my hands on his face. "But I'm not going into labor today, Antoine. And she won't dare take me before they're born. She'll be too afraid something might go wrong. Keziah wants our girls alive and well." I swallow my distaste. Antoine's own face has turned to stone. "I know how hard it is for us to talk about this," I say quietly. "But at some point, we need to talk about how you're going to turn me, Antoine."

I could also mention the mysterious vampire friends of Guidry's whom Antoine never brings up, but who seem to know an awful lot about us—or Guidry himself, whom I've barely met, though he's one of Antoine's oldest friends. Just as I haven't told Antoine what Iara explained to me about water paths, there are things he has kept quiet about too. It isn't so much that either of us is keeping secrets. It's just that there is only so much we both have room for, I guess. The twins are ours, an experience and a reality only he and I can truly understand. For the past few months, they have been all that has mattered, to either of us. The movements inside my growing belly and my strange, vivid dreams have been our own private joy, something we've wondered at and spent endless golden hours marveling over. It has been enough to know we're expecting not just one, but two miracles. I've been content to let the outside world move forward without me, and I suspect Antoine has felt the same.

That is about to change, though. Soon it won't be only our world that will concern us. Soon, the decisions we make will determine the course not only of our lives, but of those we are bringing into this world. The bodies inside my own shift and tumble as if the twins, too, are growing impatient. I think that whatever fears I have for Antoine and myself pale into insignificance when I weigh them against the future of our children.

"What is there to talk about?" Antoine steps away from me, his face grim. "We both agree you must be turned."

"Yes," I say gently. "We agreed it would happen right after the birth, as soon as the twins are free of my body." He shudders slightly, as if even my saying it aloud frightens him. "It's how it will happen that we need to discuss."

"You know how," he says harshly. "That isn't what you're asking me."

"No." I meet his eyes steadily. "It isn't." I take a deep breath. "I guess it's a question of *who*, rather than how."

Who will have to die so that I might live? Who is it that I will take into my body, to become part of my immortal soul? The slightest thought of taking a life by force horrifies me. "I haven't wanted to think about it either." I step closer to him, and this time Antoine doesn't step away. "The life that I take to become a vampire will become part of me," I say softly. "That person will be part of raising our children, Antoine. Part of me forever. We can't just pretend that doesn't matter."

One of his hands comes up and strokes the curls back from my face, twining them about the unruly pile gathered at the crown. "You're right," he says roughly, his hand cradling my head. "I know we need to talk about it, to make a plan. But I honestly don't know where to start, Harper."

My mouth twists. "It isn't like we can run an ad on Craigslist, is it?"

His own lips lift at the edges briefly. "Hardly."

The humor is gone as soon as it came, and we look at one another in the growing morning light. "We need to decide how we're going to do this, Antoine," I say quietly. "We've left it too late as it is. I can't go into this not knowing what is waiting for me on the other side. Can we agree that we have to talk about it at least?"

He nods slowly. "Agreed. But I'm not certain what talking about it will do."

I step further into his orbit, and he turns me so my back is against his chest, his hands holding my belly. I turn my head so my lips are against his jaw, just below his ear. "Talking about it will remind us that we are doing this together," I murmur against the heat of his skin. "That we aren't alone."

"Together." His arms tighten around me briefly. "Always," he murmurs.

"Always."

We stand as the day grows, and then we walk slowly up the slope together, our hands entwined.

To distract myself from my own thoughts, I head back upstairs and prop myself up on my bed. I'm no more enthusiastic about unpacking the boxes from my old Baton Rouge life than I've ever been, but the impending arrival of the twins that has made me determined to at least open the more personal of them.

"Wow. I never thought I'd see the day." Callie perches on the end of my bed, grinning at me. I shoot her a slightly mutinous look. For someone with the ability to be entirely oblivious to the need for dishes to be washed, Callie possesses what to my mind is an unhealthy predilection for order. She has been dying to get her hands on the boxes in my room for months.

"I'm only doing a few," I say warningly. "Just the personal stuff. The ones—" I break off, realizing there is no nice way of saying what I was about to.

"The boxes you wouldn't want other people opening if you die." Callie finishes the sentence for me. I open my mouth to reassure her that it's nothing of the kind, but when she raises her eyebrows, my lips twist ruefully.

"I guess." I slice open the tape. "We got left with a lot," I say apologetically. "Connor and I. First Mom's stuff, then Tessa's. I'd always planned to open Mom's boxes with Tessa, but then she got sick, and somehow, in the end, they all became one big mess that I couldn't face. I don't want to leave anyone with that mess if—" *and there it is again.* It seems there is no safe topic that doesn't somehow wind up back at my impending transformation.

"I can understand that." Callie smiles briefly, then turns with reassuringly brisk efficiency to the box. "So. Want privacy, or help?"

"Help. Definitely help." One of the things I love most about Callie is that she doesn't make a fuss.

It's oddly cathartic, pulling Mom's things out of the box. "They're Tessa's and my old christening robes." I lay the two small, tissue-paper-wrapped gowns down carefully. "I remember Mom telling me they came over from Europe with some distant ancestor. Maybe we can use them for the twins. Oh, and this is one of those dumb teaspoons that have been handed down forever and given to newborn babies. I've never understood that custom."

The time passes in reminiscence and laughter, with a few poignant moments that are made easier by Callie's earthy practicality. Toward the end of the box, I find a velvet drawstring jewelry bag. "That's odd." I hold it up, turning it over. "I thought Connor and I had all the jewelry accounted for." The bag is better quality than those from a chain store, made from plush velvet and lined with satin. The only marking on it is a curlicued letter *R.* I'm certain I've never seen it before.

I turn it upside down, and two rings fall out.

"Wow." Callie picks one up, turning it over in her hand. "These are *so* cool."

"Do you think so?" I pick up the other one, examining it curiously. It's a wide silver band overlaid with ornamental silver detail, a series of joined *fleur-de-lis.* It has an old-fashioned feel, although that may be simply because the silver is so tarnished. I look at the matching bands critically. "They need a good clean."

"What's the writing on the inside?"

"I didn't notice any." I frown at the ring, trying to see what Callie is pointing at, but I can only make out a few worn lines.

"It's French." Callie is fascinated. "Hang on." Wiping the ring carefully with a corner of her shirt, she peers at it more closely. "*Qui vivra verra,*" she reads slowly. "It means: *he who lives shall see.*"

She looks up at me with a twisted smile. "That's weirdly appropriate."

"And so strange." I turn the rings over in my hand. "I honestly have no idea where they came from. I'm sure Mom never mentioned them."

"Well, they're in with all your baby stuff, so they're probably some kind of family heirloom." I catch the faintly wistful note in Callie's voice. "It must be nice," she says quietly. "To have so much family history. Things that have been handed down for generations." She colors, and her eyes slide away from mine. When she speaks again it's with a heavy dose of her old, tough accent. "Anythin' like that in our house, would've been pawned off long ago, but I'm guessin' we didn't have nothin' anyhow. All my Momma ever said 'bout family was that we was better off without 'em. Guessin' she was right, too."

Turning away, she starts chattering on about other things, but not before I see the unshed tears glistening in her eyes. Quietly I put the rings back in the bag, and tuck them away, out of sight.

CHAPTER 2

SHAMAN

$\mathcal{T}$ate and Iara arrive at dusk, in a chauffeured car they must have taken all the way from Jackson. Because neither Antoine or Tate is remotely ostentatious with money, I often forget just how much of it they have until they do something I would normally consider ridiculously wasteful, like taking a luxury car over a hundred miles instead of asking someone to pick them up.

I'm sitting on the front porch with Callie when the sedan pulls up and the driver opens the door for Iara.

"Stay there," Iara calls when she sees me begin to struggle out of the chair. "We can come to you." My first thought is that her English has improved since she left. My second, as Tate helps her out, is that if he can't see the adoration shining from her eyes every time Iara looks at him, he needs his preternatural senses examined. And my third is that the man with them is the strangest person I've ever seen.

He's no taller than Callie. Despite his limbs being extremely thin, his chest seems oddly well-developed in proportion to the rest of him, so the overall effect is like a round, polished barrel from which poke wiry arms and legs. He's wearing a pair of

16

worn shorts that might once have been red and rubber flip-flops held together by tape. An old T-shirt with a faded beer logo on it stretches over his barrel chest. Above it, his face is completely hairless and round, with a pointed chin and oblique eyes so sunk into his head they're impossible to read. His black hair is cut in a straight line directly over his eyebrows and hangs in a sharp bob just below his ears, halfway up his jaw. He carries a long canvas package, tied around many times with what looks like palm cord, and no other baggage at all.

"This is Katiusca." Iara draws the wizened man up the stairs. The driver unloads the bags and gets back into the car, casting a last curious glance at his unusual passenger before driving away. I'm not surprised at his staring. I can't help but wonder what the airline attendants made of the odd figure.

"Hello, Katiusca." I put out my hand but the little man doesn't take it. He stares at me in open fascination, his eyes roaming all over me, and chatters away in his own language to Iara, ignoring Antoine's welcome as well as my own.

"Katiusca says you will give birth on the night of new moon, the equinox." Iara translates. "On this night the waters of the Orinoco rise. It is a time of great power. He says we must begin work immediately. He will need many hands to help."

"Well, don't hold back," mutters Antoine behind me. "Tell us what you really think. That's close enough," he says warningly, as Katiusca moves forward so he's almost standing on my toes.

Callie gives a muffled snort of laughter from somewhere off to the side, where she moved as soon as the car pulled up. She never likes being at the center of attention.

"He tries now to read what he can from Harper's body," says Iara apologetically.

"He's not much one for formalities," murmurs Tate, smiling.

"You don't say, brother." Antoine folds his arms. Callie snorts again.

"What does he mean, he will need many hands to help?" I

don't feel uneasy in Katiusca's presence—quite the opposite. I feel an odd sense of peace with him nearby. I'm not sure why. He is one of the strangest-looking people I've ever seen. And he doesn't try to make himself amiable, lacking all the social norms I'm accustomed to: smiles, polite manners. He has an abrupt demeanor and seems to totally lack any awareness of personal space. But there is something in his attitude, a kind of brusque, practical efficiency, that makes me feel as if he is here to do a job and wants only to get on with it. I find his focus oddly reassuring.

"He needs to build a platform," Iara explains, as Katiusca's flow of words continues unabated. "A special place for the kanobotuma, the carvings of our gods. A place where he dances the great serpent into being, the night you give birth. This way he will protect you and your land from anything that tries to harm you."

I like the sound of that. I will take any protection I can get.

"Wait." Antoine glances at Tate. "You mean he actually thinks he can keep Keziah out?"

The little man snorts disdainfully when he hears Keziah's name and bursts into a torrent of speech directed at Antoine. Tate nods at Iara to continue to translate. "Katiusca says his Warao magic is older and stronger than what created Keziah," she says. "Once he dances it into being, nothing, including Keziah, will pass the four-headed serpent of the Warao." Antoine raises his eyebrows in a way that suggests he is not quite so convinced of Katiusca's infallibility. I shoot him a warning glance and he rolls his eyes, but he refrains from making the acerbic comment I'm sure he longs to.

"There is more." Iara's beautiful face is somber as she looks between Antoine and me. "When he finishes dancing to our gods," she says quietly, "and after Harper has the birth, Katiusca will be Harper's sacrifice. Her first kill."

Seeing our stunned expressions, Katiusca nods his head

emphatically. He points at me, then at himself, as if his suggestion is the most natural thing in the world. I have no idea how to react, let alone how I feel. I'm so taken aback I can't begin to make sense of it.

"He's *offering* to do this?" I'm surprised my voice actually works.

"Not offering." Iara's eyes are dark and serious. "He says this must happen, if we are to defeat Keziah."

"That isn't something anyone else decides for us." Antoine's face has closed over completely, and he's eyeing the Warao man now as he would a dangerous snake in the garden.

"You don't understand." Although Katiusca is still chattering away, Iara is speaking now to Antoine and me, rather than translating for him, and her language becomes shorter, less fluent. "Katiusca is wisiratu of our tribe, like my father was. The most powerful shaman of our people. Only he is messenger between kanobotuma—the carvings—and the gods. It is he who commands the four-headed serpent, and only he who can ensure Keziah's destruction. His sacrifice is a great honor."

"I'm sure it is." Antoine is not remotely mollified by this speech. "But that doesn't mean it's an honor we will accept." His hand reaches down to mine and I grip it, hard. I don't know how I feel about Katiusca's offer, but I do know that I'm grateful Antoine is here to ensure I'm not railroaded. How do you respond to someone you don't even know telling you they will soon become a part of you—forever?

"Wait." Iara holds up one hand. Katiusca's voice has risen as we speak, and Iara leans in to listen to him. "He wants me to explain why it is so important."

"Sure." Antoine gestures derisively to a chair. "Maybe he might like to sit down. Have a drink of some kind?" Katiusca hasn't stopped speaking since he climbed out of the car.

"No." Iara waves Antoine off impatiently, the sarcasm entirely lost on her. "Katiusca is talking."

"Of course he's talking," mutters Antoine, shooting Tate a sour look. Tate's mouth twitches and I nudge Antoine with my elbow, giving Callie a quelling look to forestall another of her snorts. Antoine doesn't need the encouragement.

"Tell him to go on," I say to Iara. She smiles at me and focuses on Katiusca as she continues.

"In my tribe we have three types of shaman," Iara says. "Hoarotu, like my mother; they heal problems made by plants and animals. Then, bahanarotu. They heal problems made by foreign objects—knives, things like this. The shaman who killed my mother was bahanarotu. But the most powerful of them all is the wisiratu. He holds the magic of our ancestors, is link between the gods, and our people. Only the wisiratu can access the great magic of the Warao, the four-headed serpent that is held in the kanobotuma, and even then he needs the other three shamans to control that magic." She nods at the little man. "Katiusca says it will take all three shamans together to defeat Keziah. But he is the only shaman of his generation left. My mother is dead because the bahanarotu who killed her feared me, what power I might have, since I am the child of the union between a hoarotu and a wisiratu. Is not normal for shamans to mate, or have children together." She looks away, and I remember her telling me that was why her mother had left the village. "But," she goes on, "even if my parents did wrong when they made me, Katiusca says is much worse for one shaman to kill another." She frowns. "After my mother, the hoarotu, was murdered, I got my revenge by taking the bahanarotu as my first kill." Her eyes gleam with a flash of crimson, there and gone. "So now, only Katiusca remains from their circle of three." Iara turns back to the shaman with rapt attention. "Katiusca says it is his time to die and be reunited with them, so they may fight together in the Sky to defeat this creature, Keziah, and make right the imbalance these shamanic deaths have caused."

I try to follow what she's saying, but it's rapid and the terminology unfamiliar.

"Keziah was alive long before this generation of shamans was born," I say. "How are they responsible for the imbalance? I don't understand why this man would think it his responsibility."

Tate steps forward. "There is already a connection. The binding in your cellar," he says quietly, "was broken the same night that Iara's mother was killed." He looks at Antoine. "Katiusca was not surprised when we came to the village. He had already packed the kanobotuma. He was waiting for us."

I glance at the small man, who is nodding, his eyes still on me. For some reason I believe him. It's almost as if I can see him, sitting in some remote part of the jungle, his belongings packed, simply waiting for the moment when his skills would be called on. It's a strange feeling, as if in some way he is already part of me. I shiver.

"Katiusca already felt the force that had been freed," Iara adds, as if confirming my perception. "When he heard our story, he knew whatever had come out of your cellar was his responsibility, his fate."

"And he's willing to die for this?" Antoine still looks unconvinced.

"Of course." Iara nods. "Everything is balance. We are water people; we understand the importance of harmony to nature. If balance is not restored, the Orinoco will not flow as it should. Sickness and pain will come to our people. Katiusca has seen this magic before. He knows how to defeat it. He knew immediately, after I showed him the statue you gave me—and this." Reaching into her bag, she takes out a small stone carving. It is shaped like a horizontal S, with a face in the center that has bulging eyes and a mouth opened in a threatening cry. It is crude but malevolent, and clearly very old. Katiusca casts it another of his disdainful looks, waving it away as if it were inconsequential.

"We visited Haiti before we went to Venezuela." Tate takes over the story. "I wanted to revisit the place that I believe Keziah comes from. I met with Daniel, the colleague from the university in Port-au-Prince who helped me last time." His eyes are shadowed, and I remember he hadn't much liked compelling Daniel to take him to sacred ground the last time they met. "It seems that my last visit had some unexpected consequences. Daniel had forgotten where he took me, as I'd compelled him to. But his unconscious mind must have retained some memory of my visit, because Daniel had become obsessed with the tale of Macocael, the sentinel who failed to guard the stone people bound in the cave. He'd gone back to the mountain he'd shown me, where the sacred cave is, and the waterfall where his people worship Abatey, searching for anything that might help him understand more. He'd even summoned the courage to enter the cave itself. He said he thinks he's the first person in modern history to do so. I have no reason to doubt him. As far as I'm aware, the site is a well-kept secret. The experience of entering the cave clearly terrified Daniel. But he did find something." Tate nods at the small carving in Iara's hand. "This. He knew what it was, but not what it was doing in that cave. It was Katiusca who explained the carving's significance."

"What is it?" No matter how I try to focus on Tate's words, my eyes are continually drawn to the carving. It reminds me of something, though I can't think what. My skin tingles with the urge to touch it, while at the same time, my stomach shrivels in revulsion at the thought of doing so. It's one of the oddest sensations I've felt. Given the overprotective nature of everyone around me in the late stages of my pregnancy, I'm reluctant to let any of this show. Katiusca seems to sense its magnetic compulsion, though. He's fallen silent at last, his eyes flickering between me and the carving.

"It's a zemi, a representation of a deity, just like the statue you gave Iara," Tate explains. "The zemi you gave her, though, is a representation of Abatey herself, the most powerful of the Taíno deities, goddess of water and fertility. A goddess that has roots in Warao mythology."

"Is true." Iara nods. "The statue you give me we call Abatey, but in old times, was different." She shrugs. "My mother, she said Abatey was special for women in my family, like extra magic."

Tate gestures at Katiusca. "The Warao are a water people. They live on the banks of the Orinoco basin. Their entire lives are governed by water. Abatey might be Taíno, but her roots lie in Warao mythology, probably carried out of the Orinoco basin and into the new world at some point during the migratory period. Whereas this"—he points at the zemi in Iara's hand—"is a representation of a deity particularly associated with the Taíno people of the Caribbean. Guabancex, as the deity is known, is female and is associated with tempests, born in a geographic region where wild storms are frequent. Guabancex is worshipped as the creator and controller of those storms. She is known as *the one whose fury destroys everything*."

Katiusca is nodding eagerly. He says something to Iara, his eyes still on me.

"And you think Keziah is associated somehow with this Guabancex?" Katiusca seems to understand my question without translation and begins answering immediately, Iara rushing to keep pace with his rapid-fire speech.

"Katiusca says that what the Taíno know as 'stone people' were originally Warao—and that in the beginning, there were three of them. Keziah and two others. They were the three shamans of a Warao tribe, just like Katiusca, my mother, and her murderer were the three of this generation. When they tried to use their powers and the laws of water for their own gain, they were exiled from the tribe, and their connection to the magic of the four-headed Warao serpent cut." She listens to Katiusca for a moment. "Katiusca says perhaps they should have died for what they did, because it is against nature and our laws for shamans to use their powers for their own gain. But among our people this is a very bad thing, you understand, to kill a shaman. Even worse for one shaman to kill another. Such a crime upsets the natural balance." Her face is grave as she says this, and I can't help but wonder how she feels, having killed a bahanarotu herself. "So like this, the three shamans were not killed, but were forced to leave our water lands. Their fates were left to our gods, the Sky Walkers, to decide."

"Needless to say," Tate takes up the story, "the three of them did not die. Instead, they found their way to the Caribbean, where others of their kind had already settled." He tilts his head, just he does when discussing theories in class, and adds in a slight undertone, "Bear in mind, of course, that this is all a very long time ago, and I am relaying legend rather than fact—but according to Katiusca, in place of their connection to the Warao four-headed serpent, the three shamans then used their powers instead to channel the fury of Guabancex."

"For what?" Antoine directs his question to Tate, ignoring Katiusca completely. "And what was it they wanted in the first place? What were they trying to achieve when they were cast out?"

Iara translates the question, and Katiusca answers, but Antoine still doesn't so much as look at him, focusing instead on Iara, who in turn relays the answer in Spanish to Tate. His translation is both simple and somehow devastating.

"They were trying to make themselves immortal."

Tate frowns. "I'm unsure exactly how, but it seems that when they channeled the forces of Guabancex, they succeeded. In Guabancex, though, they had chosen a wild and unpredictable force as mistress. They bound themselves to her with one another's blood." He listens closely. Iara has stopped trying to speak English and is just translating Katiusca's incessant stream of chatter to Spanish. "It seems," says Tate, "that using such destructive force had repercussions. Guabancex granted them immortality—but living up to her reputation as the goddess of fury, she used their own magic against them. She caused the stone people to crave the very thing they had used to bind her to themselves: blood. Human blood."

He pauses for a moment, and we all look at each other, each of us, I imagine, wondering the same thing: were we hearing the origin story of all vampires?

Katiusca seems the only one unconcerned by the tale and carries on, undaunted by our silence. Eventually, Tate continues translating Iara's words.

"The blood they'd taken made them so strong that the stone people could be defeated by only two things: the power of the sun and Abatey herself." Tate frowns. "The story gets confused here. Some stories say that the trio fought amongst themselves and took different paths, others that the stone people multiplied, the three becoming many. Some tales even say the stone people themselves were worshipped by the Taíno, until their evil natures were revealed. Either way, eventually the Taíno became very afraid and did their best to destroy them, using both the power of the sun and Abatey.

"But the stone people were clever. They hid during the day and tormented the Taíno by night. Whatever good they might once have possessed had become corrupted entirely by Guabancex's wild force. They wreaked havoc—until the Taíno's own shamans worked their magic to harness the power of Guabancex in a zemi of their own." Tate nods at Iara, who holds up the stone carving. "They used it to bind the stone people into a cave. Then they worked their magic to bind the power of Abatey herself into one of their strongest warriors, Macocael, whom they set as sentinel over the cave."

"Until Macocael set them free." I remember the tale Tate had told us after his first visit to Haiti. "And became the man we called Caleb, Keziah's vampire companion, who had what we called earth magic, that helped her regenerate when she should have died."

"Exactly." Tate nods.

"Wait." Antoine is frowning at the zemi in Iara's hand. "Can I see that that?" He takes it, turning the small stone carving over with distaste before handing it back to Iara with something almost like relief.

"That is the same symbol Keziah wears as a talisman, even now," he says flatly.

No wonder the symbol is familiar. I think back to the dreams I'd had, when we first came to the mansion, before I knew anything of Keziah or what she was, the face I drew in charcoal the day Antoine came upon me on the jetty. I saw her wearing that talisman—a necklace—in my dreams. I even sketched it once, without knowing what it was. The thought chills me, like coming upon a child playing with an open flame. I had been playing with fire, and I had no idea.

It wasn't a spiral, I realize, on Keziah's talisman. It just appeared that way from a distance. Instead, it was the face of Guabancex, with curved lines spinning out of her face—like a tornado, or a hurricane.

"The Guabancex symbol is her protection against the sun." Antoine shifts uneasily, as if even the memory makes him uncomfortable. "It's more precious to her than anything else. If she wears it still, and knows how powerful it is, why would she leave the zemi behind in a cave? If she was one of the three shamans who harnessed the power in the first place, why leave behind the key to her own destruction?"

"I wondered the same thing," Tate says. "But then I thought of Daniel's fear of the cave. He would never have told me about it, let alone led me there, had I not compelled him to do so. His terror of that place was palpable. Entering it was a direct result of his frustration at the blank space in his memory caused by compulsion, and he said repeatedly that he wished he'd never gone—he thought it an evil place. Even the zemi itself he'd not so much as shown to his colleagues, for fear of their reaction. The Taíno simply do not enter that cave. Keziah and the other two stone people would have known that. Why risk taking the one thing that could destroy them outside, into a dangerous world, where something so small might be lost or used against them? Safer by far to leave it in the one place nobody dared to even speak of, let alone enter."

I shiver at the thought Daniel entering the cave. The shadow of Tate's earlier visit must have been strong indeed, to make him summon the courage to go against his every instinct.

"Tate did a deep compulsion on Daniel's mind before we left." Iara, watching me, has clearly discerned my thoughts. "He eliminated all thoughts connected to the cave, the zemi, even Tate himself."

"He would have gone insane if I hadn't compelled it all away," Tate says. "It's better this way. But I do think his fear is a good example of why Keziah and her friends left the zemi in the cave."

In the short pause that follows their story, Katiusca begins talking again. He's still looking at me, as he has from the moment he arrived, and he's still standing, the glass of water Callie silently brought him untouched on the table.

"Katiusca says that now is the time," Iara says. "The equinox is when our people perform their most powerful magic. It is when your twins will arrive—and when Keziah will return." She nods at the zemi. "We have the object in which Keziah's magic is bound. We have Katiusca, the wisiratu, the only shaman to whom even Keziah must bow, who can wield a power older and greater than the Guabancex from which her powers are drawn. And between the shamanic blood in my veins and the Abatey in yours, Harper, we have everything we need to destroy Keziah —forever."

CHAPTER 3

SERPENT

*M*y sleep is fitful. I stay awake through much of the night, then fall asleep just as dawn is coming. When I wake, Antoine is gone, the sun is high, and work has already begun beyond my window.

Antoine and Connor's trucks, both loaded with lumber, are parked down by the jetty. To my surprise, the entire pack is with them. I can see Remy ordering them about, hear their good-natured bantering as they unload lumber and set up a workspace. I'm glad they're all here, though not a little surprised. I knew Connor and Remy had struck a kind of truce. I hadn't realized the pack was comfortable enough with Connor to not only set foot on ground that sets their teeth on edge, but to work upon it with him.

Katiusca's small, wiry figure stands on the edge of the group, one finger pointing as Iara nods beside him, clearly translating his endless string of patter.

Given my size, everything takes me a great deal of time now, so it's late morning when I finally make my way downstairs. The sound of construction floats up the slope. My kitchen smells of baked goods and coffee. I discover Callie and

Cass there, chatting away over plates of sandwiches and muffins.

"You shouldn't be up!" Callie leaps to her feet as I come in. I wave her away.

"I'm not ill, Callie. Just pregnant." There's no need for me to remain standing, but for some strange reason, ever since it's become hard, I feel as if I should make myself do it. I'm sure a psychologist would have a field day with that.

"*So* pregnant." Cass eyes the mountain of my belly. "You look like a drunk horse. Or a floundering ship."

"How poetic," I say dryly.

"Whatever." Callie shrugs. "Not something that should be walking around. Sit down. You're huge. Like, so huge you look like you're going to explode. It makes me nervous just watching you." I want to argue with her, but the reality is that even a few minutes on my feet makes everything hurt. I make it to the chair she's holding and collapse down on it, raising my feet gratefully onto the stool she pushes in front of me. I wish I was one of those elegant pregnant women, draped in white, with a polite bump that looks like a well-mannered guest. Instead, I'm wearing a cotton dress that has more in common with a tent than haute couture, despite its artful cut and faded aqua coloring. There's nothing polite about the mound of my belly, and the twins are not so much guests as conquerors who have made my body their own.

"Enormous," Callie mutters again, then reddens when she sees my face. I'm taking the muffin she offers just as Antoine comes in.

"You're up," he says, not altogether happily.

"Yes. I am." I take a bite of the muffin, my eyes daring him to say a word about how I should be in bed.

"I might take these down to the boys." Callie reaches for a tray of sandwiches, looking warily between Antoine and me.

"I'll join you," says Cass hastily. A moment later, the kitchen is empty but for the two of us. Antoine leans against the sink. Crossing one leg over the other and folding his arms, he regards me silently as I eat the muffin. He says nothing until I reach for my cup, at which point he moves with vamp speed to whisk it out of my hand and fill it with the herbal tea Iara has me drinking in place of real, heavenly coffee. I sigh. There's no point arguing.

But, oh, I miss coffee.

"Where are they building the platform?" I head off the inevitable questions about how I feel. The truth is, I find it so hard to move I do actually appreciate the help, but I'm so uncomfortable and frustrated that I feel irritable, all the time.

"Right between your night garden and the water garden." Antoine casts me a slightly wary look. "We didn't have a whole lot of choice. Our new favorite shaman is giving the orders. I wanted to wake you and check that it was okay, but you were sleeping."

"It's fine." The idea of having a shamanic platform built right by my garden isn't a prospect that fills me with joy. But I know the magic that lies in that garden, and if I do, no doubt Katiusca feels it too. I force a smile. "It's the best place for it." Antoine visibly relaxes. He sips his coffee, still watching me. "Go on, then," I say eventually. "What is it?" As if I didn't already know what was coming.

"I didn't want to raise it last night, because you were tired, and there was so much to take in."

"You're worried about Katiusca being the sacrifice." I finish the thought for him, and he nods. Before I can continue, Tate and Guidry simultaneously appear at either door to the kitchen, Tate from the rear slope, Guidry leaping up the front porch steps. They both freeze, faces closing over. They turn as one toward us and nod hello, neither acknowledging the other at all.

"Guidry." I smile as the tall, rangy man leans against the open front-door frame, as if poised for a quick exit. "I imagine you had something to do with the wolves being here today. Thank you."

"It's nothing." His grim expression doesn't alter, and he doesn't take his eyes from Tate. I sigh inwardly. I know there is old animosity between the two, going back to the days when they existed in separate Natchez clans, on either side of the river. I'm not certain what the exact cause of the hostility is. Tate left soon after our wedding, and this is the first time I've seen them in close quarters since that night. It's blatantly obvious that time has done nothing at all to lessen whatever old grudge lies between them.

"Antoine." Tate nods toward the back door. "Connor asked if you'd come down and help him make sense of what Katiusca is asking for. Also, Harper, there'll be a delivery from the lumber yard coming sometime soon, if you could send them on down back." Smiling at me, Tate heads straight for the door, not so much as looking at Guidry, whose flint-eyed stare follows him all the way out. The position of my chair means I can see Tate's face as he passes through the doorway, his back to the rest of the room. His eyes are unguarded, and right before he moves out of sight I see an expression in them, and a particular flush on his cheeks, that takes me by surprise. I've seen Tate concerned. I've seen him angry. But this is something different: Tate looks ashamed.

Before I have time to think on it, Antoine steps forward. "We'll finish our conversation in a moment?" He touches my shoulder, squeezing it briefly when I nod. "You stay here and rest. Guidry—" He looks at his old friend, who waves him away.

"I'll stay with her," Guidry says in his laconic way. "You go on, now." He tilts his head toward the door, and Antoine's face relaxes into the lopsided smile I rarely see him grant anyone other than me. He touches my shoulder again and is gone.

"We don't see enough of you." I smile at Guidry, pushing the plate of muffins toward him. "You should come here more often. Antoine enjoys it when you do."

"I've been much occupied with training up that young wolf pack, of late." His accent has altered since his return, deepened from a more refined, almost British accent with occasional lapses into Spanish and French, to more of a Louisiana drawl. Even so, it retains something otherworldly, a slight inflection here and there which makes me think alternately of Scarlett O'Hara and big dresses, or Pride and Prejudice. His voice has a slight rasp that can sound sardonic, savage, or seductive, depending on his mood. I've found myself fascinated by Guidry from the moment I met him, mainly because he offers a rare window into Antoine that even Tate cannot. Tate and Antoine were estranged for much of the past three centuries. Guidry, on the other hand, knew Antoine throughout that time. Though they may not have spent every moment together, they clearly share more history than Antoine does with anyone else. Guidry is the only friend Antoine invited to his wedding, and I've never seen him so at ease with anyone as he is in Guidry's company.

"I take it they're building some kind of temple out back?" Guidry nods down toward the construction site.

"Yes. Tate and Iara brought back a shaman from Venezuela who says he knows how to fight off Keziah." Guidry's face darkens. Too late, I realize I've invoked the one name guaranteed to make him angry. "I'm sorry. I know you and Tate have —differences."

Guidry's laugh is more a savage rasp. "You could put it that way, sure." In what I suspect is an unconscious gesture, one of his hands comes up, the thumb stroking the thick white line at his throat. A horrible suspicion strikes me.

"Did Tate give you that scar?" I say abruptly, staring at it. "Is that why you hate him so much?"

Guidry's face is cold, his eyes like flint. "I think it's best if we talk of something else." The deliberate way he sips his coffee tells me the conversation is closed. A short silence follows. When Guidry speaks again, his eyes are warmer, and I can tell he's making a deliberate effort to soften his voice. "How are you feeling, Harper?" He nods at my belly. "You must be close now." It's a normal-enough question, but there's a genuine concern in his voice I find touching. Whatever lies between him and Tate, I think, is his business. It shouldn't take away from his obvious care not only for Antoine, but for me, as Antoine's wife.

"I'm okay." I wriggle uncomfortably. "Though I have to admit, I'm still trying to take in everything that Katiusca—the shaman—told us last night."

"I can imagine." Guidry nods. "Antoine called me early this morning, told me what the little man said." I hide my surprise. Antoine and I have barely discussed it. His confiding in Guidry speaks volumes for the esteem in which he holds his friend.

"What do you think?" I'm genuinely interested in his answer. Given Guidry's taciturn nature, I'm expecting, at best, cynical reticence.

Guidry's eyes meet mine directly. "I think it's the kind of offer you don't turn away." He shrugs, his eyes dropping to my belly. "If it will help protect—" he breaks off abruptly, seeming uncharacteristically flustered. "If it will protect all of you, then it's the right thing, don't you think?"

I'm less interested in what he's saying than whatever it is he was going to say. I want to press him further, but we're interrupted by a flatbed truck pulling up outside. It's from the lumber yard, I see, from the writing on the side. A door slams, and a moment later a bulky man appears in the open door, clipboard in hand. "I got a delivery here for a Mr. Garrison?" The man casts Guidry a wary glance and takes a step back.

"Oh, sure." I smile at him. "If you want to take the truck on down back, Tate's expecting you." The man tips his hat, glances at the menacing figure by the door again, and walks back to his truck. I turn back to Guidry, but whatever I was going to ask him dies in my throat. His face is a savage mask, his eyes the chips of flint from earlier, and I half expect him to growl rather than talk when he opens his mouth.

"Garrison?" He says fiercely, the rasp in his voice so pronounced it is like a snarl. "That's the name he goes by?"

"Tate?" I say tentatively. "Yes. Garrison is the surname he uses."

Guidry springs away from the doorframe and strides out onto the porch, then back in again, as if he's fighting to get himself under control.

"Harper." I close my eyes briefly as I hear Tate's voice come through from the back porch, the sound of his footsteps on the boards. "Was that the flatbed I saw?" He halts abruptly as he comes into the kitchen and sees Guidry glaring at him. "I thought you'd gone."

"I'm sure you did," says Guidry harshly. "Can't imagine you'd be accepting deliveries under the name Garrison if you thought I'd be here, now would you, *Serpent*?"

"I never pretended to the role of Serpent." Tate's voice is not quite steady.

"No, you did not." Guidry's voice drips with contempt. "You never led your people. You just waged war as an army of one instead and let the rest of us suffer for it." He takes a step closer to Tate, dropping his voice to a menacing growl. "And you take the name Garrison, Takatoka? Like you needed something to remember it by?" He touches the scar on his throat again. "There are those of us who have no such need, old friend."

Tate's face flames beneath the olive skin, but he doesn't look away from Guidry's eyes, nor does he take a step backward. A tense silence is broken by Antoine's voice. "Tate," he says quietly. "They need your signature on the paperwork." Tate glances at me. His eyes slide away, and for the second time, I see shame in them. He turns and disappears without another word.

"Guidry." Antoine's voice is low and calm. The wolf looks at him, the savagery slowly fading from his eyes. Guidry raises his hands in a gesture of surrender.

"I know, I know." He backs toward the porch. "I'm leaving."

"No."

Guidry halts.

"I was going to ask if you'd help Harper upstairs," Antoine says, "and stay with her a while. I'm going to be busy out back, and I thought she could use the company."

Guidry looks as taken aback as I feel. "You want me to stay?"

Antoine's mouth twists. "So long as you're not planning to eat my brother for breakfast, then yes, I do."

Guidry folds his arms belligerently in a gesture so reminiscent of Antoine's it makes me half smile. "Why?"

"Because Harper and I need every one of our friends at our side," says Antoine quietly. "And regardless of the past, Guidry, you and Tate are the two I most trust to have there." There's a long silence during which neither man moves. Finally Guidry exhales, raking a hand through his hair.

"Fine," he says curtly. "But keep him away from me, Marigny. And tell him not to use that damned name in my presence."

Antoine casts me a wry smile and the ghost of a wink as he turns. "Go upstairs and rest," he says. "Something tells me you're going to need it."

CHAPTER 4

HISTORY

"So," Guidry says as he helps me up the stairs. "I run by here on the other side of the river, some mornings. I notice that young girl who lives here training on the jetty. Callie, is it?"

"Callie. Yes." I wonder if I'm supposed to be pretending nothing just happened downstairs. "She was taught martial arts back in Memphis. Trains every morning now. Rain, hail, or shine."

"That's some sword she has."

"It's Japanese, I believe. A gift from her old teacher."

"Well, she's good with it."

"Yes, she is." We've reached the top of the stairs. I'm panting hard, but that isn't the reason I stop. I turn to Guidry. "Are you going to explain what happened down there?"

He clicks his tongue and looks away, hands loosely on his hips. "Some things are best left, maybe."

"Maybe." I fold my arms over my belly and stare at him. "But if you're going to be here when my babies are born, I think I'd rather have the truth."

Guidry's face sharpens. "There's nothing that will get in the way of me protecting those girls."

His answer comes so hard and fast it takes me aback a little. Seeming to realize his response was unusual, he shoots me a sideways glance. "They're Antoine's daughters." He shrugs, smiling wryly. "Which makes them about as close to a miracle as anything can be." I remember Antoine saying almost exactly the same thing. It's a touching reminder of just how similar the two men are.

"I'd like to know what it is that caused the rift between you and Tate." I figure that asking directly can't hurt. Guidry exhales slowly, whistling between his teeth as he does, his eyes looking somewhere over my shoulder. "If you don't tell me, I'll just ask Tate. And if he won't tell me, Antoine will. It's easier if you just come out with it."

"Ha." Guidry ducks his head, smiling wryly in his twisted way. "Well, then." He gestures to a chair on the landing. "Perhaps you should sit."

"I'm good. The next time I lower myself down will be on my bed, and once I'm there, I'm likely to be asleep in ten seconds. I'll stand."

"Well, then," Guidry says again. He's clearly at a loss for where to start.

"Given your reaction to his name, I'm guessing whatever happened has something to do with Tate's attack on the French garrison, just after he was turned." Guidry looks at me in surprise. I meet his eyes. "Tate told me about it."

"He told you?" Guidry's eyes narrow. "How much did he tell you, exactly?"

"Tate said he massacred an entire garrison of French soldiers." I use the word deliberately, and Guidry flinches slightly. "He told me that afterward, the French took a terrible revenge on the Natchez. They killed many, members of Tate's own family among them."

"Well, then. He told the truth." Guidry leans over the banister, his hands linked loosely together. "He left out a part, though. The French's revenge was largely taken on our side of the river, not his. And one of those family members he spoke of was married to me." He turns flat grey eyes to mine. "My wife and I had two children. A girl and a boy."

I'm shocked into silence.

Guidry, seeing my face, nods grimly. "The French came to our village at night. They killed everyone they found and burned our houses. I fought back. We all did. I stood in the doorway of my home, my wife and children inside, and cut down four French soldiers before they overpowered me. They made me watch as they killed my children, and then my wife. I watched each of them scream in agony as they died. The French waited until the last scream died away, and then they cut my throat." He touches the scar. "Our houses were made of wattle and daub. They burned easily. The French soldiers set mine alight and left me for dead. And so I would have been, had Antoine not come across me soon after." He meets my eyes. "Antoine heard my cries. He walked through flames to rescue me, even though fire kills those of his kind. He pulled me free, and he gave me his blood to heal. And then . . ." He holds his hands out.

"You became a wolf." I struggle for words. Even after all this time, I can see the memory of the flames in his eyes as Guidry tells the story. "I'm sorry, Guidry." I put my hand on his arm. He tenses but doesn't pull away. "I understand why you can't forgive that."

How could anyone, ever, forgive such a thing?

"Perhaps I could have forgiven it, with time. I was young, barely twenty." He stares into the distance. "I'd known Antoine before any of this. Back when he was trapping animals inland, working with my people. He was a friend, and I trusted him. He told me about his kind, about how hard it is for them, in the time after they turn, to manage the twin sides of their personality. Antoine explained that Takatoka had been split in two—become two people—and that he was at war within himself. Perhaps I could understand how that made him attack the French garrison. And like I said, perhaps I could have forgiven that."

"But you didn't," I say. "You still haven't forgiven it. Why?"

"Because the deaths of my wife and children weren't the only consequences of Takatoka's actions. After the French attack on my clan, there were none left who knew our stories. Every warrior, every elder, died in the attack. All those who knew our spirit stories were gone. Takatoka took from me any chance to ask about what I was, what I'd become after taking Antoine's blood. When I turned, became wolf, I knew none of my kind nor anything of how to be what I was. It took nearly a lifetime of travel before I found any others—and even then, they were different, not as I am." He meets my eyes. "Throughout that lifetime of searching, it was Antoine who helped me. As for Takatoka—he never once looked back. During that lifetime, he was consumed with resentment toward Antoine. And if he wasn't any kind of warrior when he was a man, he certainly made up for it afterward. The attack by the French was not the only mess of Takatoka's that Antoine cleaned up. The only reason I never killed him was out of respect for Antoine, who asked me not to. Whether that selfish ba—" His voice breaks off and he shakes his head. "Excuse me. I guess I've just never understood why Antoine bothers with Takatoka. I lost track of him many years ago, and I never bothered to seek him out again."

Knowing something of the Maker's bond that exists between Antoine and Tate, I have perhaps more understanding of the complex dynamic between them, but I don't want to speak out of turn. And I need time to think about what Guidry has said. "Whatever the reason," I say, my hand still on his arm, "Antoine and Tate are as close now as they ever were when they were human. The only other person I've seen Antoine trust as he does Tate is you, Guidry." I press his arm gently. "And he meant what he said. We are going to need both you and Tate. Whatever happens, we are going to need our friends close when the time comes. I hope you and Tate can find a way to put aside your differences." His arm is tense under my touch, but after a moment, he covers my hand with his own. "I told you I'd be here," he says roughly. "You have my word, Harper, as your husband will always have my loyalty. I'm sworn to protect you and your daughters. I will do so, with my life, if I must."

Given the emotional undercurrents, his intensity is not really surprising. Suddenly flattened by exhaustion, as happens so quickly lately, I'm too wiped out to think on it all anymore, so I excuse myself to go into my room and lie down, leaving him on the landing.

"I'll be here," he says quietly, as I close my door. "Right outside, should you need me."

SACRIFICE

*A*fter another disturbed night, I spend the next day struggling to eat, trying and failing to sleep, unable to stick with anything much. I can't focus on a book. If I try to sketch, my hands feel clumsy and nothing is clear. I get urges to clean up, then find myself exhausted as soon as I start. As seems to be the pattern lately, I get a sudden burst of energy at dusk, and when Antoine comes upstairs, I'm sitting on the window seat looking down at the construction site by the river.

"Our new guest is a hard taskmaster," Antoine says as he comes into the room. "He'll have that platform done by tomorrow's end, the way he's going." His voice has a certain edge to it, as it always does when he speaks of Katiusca, and I notice he also never calls the shaman by name.

"You don't like him."

"I don't trust him." Antoine sits on the window seat opposite me, stretching his legs out on the other side of mine and crossing them at the ankles. "There's too much we don't know, Harper. Keziah has been missing all these months. We even suspected she'd gone to South America, to try to find out more about Iara. What if she found the shaman before we did and compelled him to do her bidding? What if he is under her control?" He is frowning, staring out the window as if he is mentally running through all the possible scenarios, and not for the first time.

"I know you better than that." I touch his leg gently. "There's no way you or Tate would have let him anywhere near me unless you'd compelled him to tell you the truth."

"He's a shaman, Harper. There's no guarantee he can't withstand compulsion." Antoine's eyes are hard grey, an expression I know well. He's on the defensive, in warrior mode.

"Do you have any reason to think he is resisting it? Have you found any evidence of frankincense?"

"Tate and Iara have watched his every move. If there was any in his system, it's long gone. And Tate—tested his blood. It's clean." It takes me a moment to realize that by *testing*, he means tasting. Antoine's lips twitch. "Yes," he murmurs. "We wanted to be sure."

"Well, then." I try for a nonchalance I don't feel. As the day of my inevitable transformation comes closer, I'm finding it harder to speak of drinking blood with the same detachment I once did. By the tightening of Antoine's mouth, the change hasn't gone unnoticed. "If you know he's clean, then you're as sure as you can be that he's telling the truth."

"Then you want to go through with this." I can tell Antoine is trying for a neutral tone, but I know him too well. His voice is flat, with a hard edge.

"I know you aren't comfortable with it," I begin.

"Comfortable!" In one preternaturally swift movement, Antoine is on his feet, pacing the bedroom in long strides. "No, Harper. I'm not *comfortable*." He stops, raking a hand through his hair impatiently as he faces me. "When I thought about who might become a part of you, I had thought of someone like Noya. Someone gentle and wise. Like you, perhaps, in nature. Someone with qualities and values similar to your own, whom you could live with in harmony. Not something like—*him*." He stares out the window, where Katiusca's wiry figure is moving quickly through the growing dusk, darting here and there with mercurial swiftness.

I try and fail to imagine that odd, wizened creature becoming a part of me, something I carry inside myself, forever. Even the thought of it makes me inwardly shudder.

"Don't try to tell me you don't feel the same way." Antoine is watching me closely.

"I can't." I meet his eyes. "But tell me you didn't feel the same way at the prospect of taking the medicine woman into your own skin. And look at what a miracle that has proven to be, for all of us. You can bind the sun into new vampires. Defy Keziah. All of that, because she sacrificed herself for you."

"That was different." Antoine glares at me. "When I agreed to be turned, I didn't understand what it would mean to absorb her into my soul. I don't think she did either, not truly. It's not the same for you. We know what will happen. We have the chance to do it differently, to choose carefully. Someone not so strange, from such a different world." He looks away, his mouth working.

"What is it?" With an effort, I turn and push myself to my feet, coming over to stand before him. The last light on the horizon catches the gold in his eyes, highlighting the dark shadows behind them. I touch his face, rough with a day's growth. "What aren't you saying, Antoine?"

He is still under my touch, barely breathing, and when he finally speaks, his voice is low and full of an odd pain. "Has it occurred to you that it is not only you who must live with this shadow in your soul?" His eyes seem to retract, becoming indistinct as night falls. "After you turn, Harper, you will no longer be alone in your body. That shaman will be inside you also. When I hold you, he will be there." He covers my hand with his own, his eyes searching mine. "When I look at you, he will be there, behind your eyes. He will be in our every conversation." A savage look crosses his face. "He will be in our bed, Harper."

I feel sick and dizzy, cold inside. It's hard to remain standing. Antoine nods, his face hardening. "Now you begin to see," he says grimly. "This isn't something you simply move on from. It's permanent. As fixed as anything ever can be. Our *always* will no longer be ours alone, Harper. He will be part of it, too."

I nod, swallowing, trying to maintain my equilibrium. When Antoine leads me back to the window seat, I don't argue. I sit down on it heavily. I stare out the window, but night has fallen, and Katiusca is no longer visible in the darkness.

"No," I say as Antoine moves to turn on the lamp. The fairy lights on my four-poster glow softly, casting all the light I want just now. "I hadn't thought of what this would mean for you." I take his hand, turning it over in mine. "For us." He doesn't say anything, just watches me for a while. Outside an owl calls, long and haunting. A restless breeze stirs the live oak, Spanish moss trailing like ghosts under the growing stars. "Do you want me to refuse his offer?" I say finally. "Try to find someone else?"

"It isn't my decision to make." Antoine's voice is strained. "I wish it was, Harper. But no matter how I feel about it, this is something only you can decide."

"We said we'd discuss it together."

"And we are. Ultimately, though, this will be your choice. Only you know what lies within your soul, what you can take into it. You asked that we talk about it, and I'm doing my best to be honest about what I feel. But I won't try to force you either way." He strokes my hand softly.

"When you took the medicine woman Atsila into your body," I say slowly, "she gave you power. Power to resist Keziah, to wield sun magic. She made you different than others of your kind." He nods. "I guess I am hoping that Katiusca will give me something similar," I say. "Not for me, Antoine."

"For our daughters."

I nod. "I'm afraid of what Keziah will try. I'm afraid I won't be strong enough to defy her, to fight her off. Everything Katiusca has said tells me that he understands what I'm going to face, and that he's confident he can help me. Turning away the best opportunity we might have to protect our girls, simply because I don't feel . . . *drawn* to him, seems not only selfish. It seems irresponsible."

Antoine's head moves slowly in understanding. "I hear that. Equally, what if that feeling you have, of not being drawn to him, is a warning? Should you heed that, perhaps, above all else?"

"Did you feel drawn to the medicine woman?"

Antoine lifts his shoulders helplessly. "I felt nothing. I honestly don't recall feeling anything for her, either way, until I took her into my body. I wasn't trying to feel anything, I guess. I didn't know it would matter."

"Then perhaps that is how it is. Until they become part of us, we can't know what it will be. I don't feel repelled by Katiusca. I just don't feel a bond with him." I'm grateful for the gloom so that Antoine can't see the expression in my eyes. "Yes," I say softly, "you're right, Antoine. When I think of taking Katiusca into my body, I feel . . . uneasy. Ill, even. But I feel that way about *anyone* inhabiting my body with me, becoming part of my soul. It terrifies me." My fingers close around his. "It's also what I signed up for when I married you. It's what you and Tate have both endured, what Cass has. How can I shy away from it? I chose this life, Antoine. I have to find the strength to do what that life asks of me." I touch his face with my other hand. "We both do," I say quietly.

Antoine is still, his face shadowed so I can't read it. When he speaks, his voice is tired and resigned. "Then you're determined it will be him?"

"I think it must be."

Briefly his fingers tighten on mine, then, just as quickly, he releases my hand altogether. Antoine moves slightly away from me. It hurts somewhere deep inside, like an old wound reopening. I had thought the time when we were separate beings was gone, behind us. It's painful to think we may face that again. "Don't pull away from me," I whisper, the words scraping against my throat. "I need you, Antoine. I need this to be something we do together."

"I know that." The pain in his voice hurts as much as his withdrawal. "I want that, too. I just have to find a way to —accept it."

"Accept me," I say sadly. "You mean you need to find a way to accept what I will be."

There's a long silence.

"We'll find a way," Antoine says, but this time his reassurance sounds hollow to me, and I can't derive a shred of comfort from it.

"Sure." My voice is as empty as his. "Sure we will, Antoine."

Night grows, and eventually I go back to bed. When I wake a few hours later, Antoine has gone hunting, and the bedroom is empty.

I lie awake in the still hours, and all I can think is that neither of us so much as mentioned the word *always*—other than to say it was no longer ours alone.

BOUCHER

For the next couple of days, Antoine and I move around one another much like the proverbial ships in the night, rarely meeting for long enough to exchange anything more than the most basic of conversation. His days are spent helping Katiusca construct the platform, which is now an entire pagoda-style building, with four large round pillars at each corner. He spends his nights hunting with either Guidry or Tate. Depending on which one, the other is in the house. This evening, Tate and Antoine have gone together. I eat in the kitchen with Guidry, Iara, and Callie and go back upstairs soon after. I fall into another uneasy sleep before nightfall, which is disturbed by urgent footsteps pounding excitedly up the stairs.

"Harper!" Callie's excited voice tugs me back to the surface. "Jeremiah will be home this weekend! Oh," she says, as she comes into the room to find me on the bed. "Were you sleeping?"

"It's okay." I struggle upwards groggily. "I don't really sleep anymore, so much as swim in and out of consciousness." I lean back against the pillows, eyeing Callie from under half-closed lids. "It will be nice to have Jeremiah home."

As I come blearily to awareness, the events of a few nights ago reassert themselves, worry and fear creeping in over my happiness at Jeremiah's return. The horrible silence between Antoine and me looms, a dark, unwelcome gulf. I force myself to focus on Callie in a bid to avoid thinking about it. "You must be looking forward to seeing him."

"Yeah, sure." Callie's carefully constructed expression of nonchalance wouldn't pass the loosest scrutiny.

"But?" I prompt, aware that I'm shamelessly exploiting the conversation to distract myself from my own thoughts.

"It's not like Jeremiah and I are . . . seeing each other or anything." Callie colors uncomfortably. "We don't, like, talk every day or anything."

"But you have talked."

"A bit. Especially about, you know." She nods at my belly.

I smile wryly. "I bet."

"Yeah." Callie settles on the bed and looks out the window, clearly unsure of what she wants to say. "Anyhow. It will be good to see his skinny butt again." For a moment I'm tempted to make the observation that Jeremiah's butt seemed to have filled out considerably when he came home for Christmas, but remembering the rather awkward silence between the two at the table, I think better of it. Avery spent Christmas in the bayou with Remy, thank the stars. Jeremiah hadn't seemed so sad about that, I'd thought at the time. I suspect that a few months away at college had served to both remind Avery of how much she missed Remy, and Jeremiah how much he missed Callie. Christmas had been a little stiff and formal, but spring break, I think, might just be the welcome thaw Callie and Jeremiah need.

"Have you and Antoine decided where you're going to have the birth?" Callie changes the subject—obviously a welcome relief for her, but not so much for me. "I saw the room Connor and Antoine renovated two doors down from yours. It looks like a state-of-the-art hospital suite."

"Antoine compelled the obstetrician to help him, then bought absolutely everything she might need. It's not as though there are a lot of options." I try for a smile, but I know it's a poor effort. "I can't go to a hospital, in case . . . well."

"In case the twins come out . . . different?"

"Different." I stifle a slightly hysterical laugh. "Yes."

"Yeah. I guess half-vampire, time-traveling babies might freak the doc out a little."

"We don't know if they're half vampire."

"But we do know they're time travelers."

"The reality is, Callie, that we don't actually know much at all." I stare at the fabric hanging over my four-poster bed. "Iara is going to help deliver them. She's used to helping with births. Antoine has compelled my obstetrician to be available and close by, in case of complications, and there's also a trained nurse on standby. But we're going to try to have them here, at home, without outside help." There's no need to tell Callie the other reasons why we want to keep the birth as private as possible. She already knows we're expecting any number of uninvited, unwelcome, and highly dangerous guests. It's hardly going to be a safe environment for humans. I'm already worried about Callie and Jeremiah, and I know Remy has outright forbidden Avery from being anywhere near the mansion when I go into labor.

When Callie takes my hand, I let her. We sit there in silence for a while. I like this about Callie, that I can just be whatever I need to be. She doesn't fuss, just like Connor.

After a minute, she gets up and goes to the far wall of my room, to the remaining boxes we haven't dealt with. "Want me to clear some of this mess for you?"

"Seriously?" I prop myself up on one arm and look at the

chaos dubiously. "I know we started, but I just got overwhelmed by it all. Are you sure you want to keep going?"

"I like sorting stuff out." Callie shrugs.

"Wow. You have my respect." I smile at her. "Then by all means—have at it." I flop back down on the pillows, exhaustion overwhelming me. Callie starts working away, holding things up so I can see them, then sorting them into piles. As I did last time, I find it strangely comforting, lying there watching her. It's poignant to see clothes I haven't worn since we lived in Baton Rouge. They belong to a life so far away from this one, it seems like a foreign land. I feel an ache for that time, when I was just Harper Ellory, teenage girl. Not Harper Marigny, wife to a vampire, mother to time-traveling twins, and about to share her body with a South American shaman.

"What's this?" Callie holds up a large, cream box and traces the embossed words on the lid. "Maison de Lysette," she reads, her accent perfect. Callie's language skills never cease to amaze me.

"I swear, you're wasted on pre-med. Your French is as perfect as your Spanish." Callie turns red with pleasure at the compliment but doesn't say anything. "It was the box my wedding dress came in."

"Your dress is so beautiful." Callie opens the box and frowns when she finds it empty. "Where is it?"

"Zipped up in a bag in the closet. But I didn't want to throw the box away." Callie passes it to me, and I run my hands over the raised writing. "Antoine said Madame Lysette is an old friend of his, though I don't know how, exactly, or from when."

"I can probably answer that." We both look up, startled, to find Guidry's large figure ranged across the doorway. His face wears its customary insouciant smile, underlaid with the predatory darkness I always sense around him.

"You knew this Madame Lysette?"

"I did. I do." He throws me his trademark wolfish grin. Lounging there against the doorframe, arms crossed over his chest, he reminds me so much of Antoine that my heart aches. There's something of Antoine's own watchfulness in Guidry's manner, a quiet power that is lethal and quiet rather than overt. The difference is on the surface. Guidry is inevitably sardonic, full of sharp ripostes and easy, if barbed, humor.

"Tell us about her." Callie's eyes are shining. She and Jeremiah, more than any of us, are fascinated by the centuries of history lived by Antoine, Tate, and Guidry.

"Hm." Guidry's smile becomes cryptic. His eyes rest on Callie for a moment, sizing her up, as if he is considering how much to share. I'm reminded again of how similar he and Antoine are, the many layers they have learned to build against the world. "I guess I can tell you a little."

"Come in." Eager for distraction, I gesture at the easy chair in the corner. "Join us."

"Erm . . ." He looks over his shoulder uncomfortably, as if worried about propriety. "I'm not certain your husband would appreciate my being in your bedroom."

"It's fine." I'm a little amused by his concern. "Callie is here as chaperone. And we can leave the door open." He moves hesitantly into the room, clearly not entirely certain he's doing the right thing, and perches uneasily on the chair in the corner. "Tell us about Madame Lysette."

"*D'accord.*" Guidry clears his throat, seemingly unaware he's just used a French phrase. "I first met Madame Lysette in Paris —in 1793."

"*La Révolution!*" Callie's eyes are as wide as saucers.

"*La Terreur,*" Guidry corrects her. "Yes, the French Revolution. But the years of The Terror—they were different. Terrible years." His eyes settle on Callie's face, that odd intensity back in them. "To be on the streets of Paris in 1793 was to risk death at every turn," he says. "From every corner. Nowhere was safe from the revolutionaries, especially if they suspected someone of being of aristocratic birth. The streets ran with blood."

"Why were you there?" Callie asks. She is clearly fascinated. Knowing how much she loves all things historical, I think it's kind of Guidry to respond to her questions with such detail.

Guidry shrugs. "I'd come to Europe on a ship many years before. There wasn't a great deal left for me here." His eyes flicker to me. His face hardens momentarily, and I realize he's speaking of the years following the massacre of his family, when he was searching for others of his kind. He looks back at Callie. "In France, I discovered others like me. I made friends, and a home, of sorts. Many of my friends were also . . . different." His mouth twists into a sardonic smile. "Much like your little community here, for example."

"After the Revolution began, we found ourselves in danger. Many of my friends were aristocrats, or, like me, had made themselves such over the centuries. Our lives were disrupted, our lands and wealth threatened. While charismatic, men such as Robespierre and, later, Napoleon, were not the most likable of fellows." His smile is both wicked and slightly sinister. "I had nothing to lose. I supported the principles of the Revolution, but not tyranny. Some of the aristocrats I knew, and considered friends, were human, and they became targets of the madness. After they were executed, I decided to help those who wished to escape." He tilts his head to one side, his eyes still on Callie. "I wasn't the only one. Madame Lysette was part of our network. She had an establishment in a district of Paris known as Filles-Saint-Thomas. It was in the Rue Vivienne." He nods at Callie. "I understand you speak a little French. Do you know where that is?"

"Filles-Saint-Thomas?" Callie repeats the name, smiling. "No. I've never been to Paris."

"It's in the 2nd arrondissement, near the Place Vendôme. Madame Lysette's was in a small street, Rue Vivienne, just off Boulevard Haussmann." He reels the names off easily, as if expecting Callie to understand.

"La Rue Vivienne, en Filles-Saint-Thomas," Callie repeats, savoring the sound of the words.

"*Eh bien!*" Guidry tilts his head in approval. "Your accent is excellent." Callie's face turns pink with pleasure. "I remember the place well," he continues. "Those of us who worked with Madame Lysette did not enter from the Rue Vivienne, however. There was another door, a tunnel, that came up into her cellar. The entry to that was through a knife maker's shop, in a nearby street." Reaching behind him, he pulls out a gleaming blade, with a carved wooden handle. "I carry one of his blades still. I met Duval, the knife maker, on my first day in Paris. He was one of Madame Lysette's friends. It was he who introduced me to her—and told me the password I would need to enter the cellar from the tunnel that ran from his shop to her establishment."

"It sounds so romantic." Callie's eyes are shining.

"Ha!" Guidry's laugh is a harsh bark. "That is the grand deception of all war—that it sounds romantic after the fact." His smile fades. "When one is fighting it, I assure you, the romance is not so obvious."

Going by Callie's shining eyes, however, this remark has gone unheeded. "This Madame Lysette," she asks eagerly. "She was a dressmaker?"

Guidry laughs. "No, she was not. Hers was an establishment of quite a different kind. The ladies at La Rose were famous throughout Paris."

Callie's eyes widen. "You mean she was . . ."

"Yes," says Guidry, still laughing at her shock. "She was, indeed, although by then she had risen to the role of proprietess and no longer worked the floor herself. Her establishment was a favorite of politicians, which meant she had excellent access to information. The knife maker, Duval, was part of her network. He met men like me, *et voila*, he would take them to La Rose and introduce them to Madame Lysette and her courtesans. Then, if deemed suitable, they would be taken into her confidence, as I was." Callie is avidly hanging on his every word. Guidry's mouth twists into a wry smile. "We each had a password of our own," he says, clearly indulging her. "I still recall mine, even all these years later. I chose it myself. It was *Boucher*."

The word means nothing to me, but Callie frowns and gives him a quizzical smile. "Boucher? As in an actual butcher, or like the painter?"

Guidry raises his eyebrows. "*Très bien!* You know the painter, then?"

Callie shrugs impatiently. "I did an art history class for extra credit back in Memphis."

Guidry shakes his head, still smiling, his eyes resting curiously on Callie. "Well, there was a reason for it—a story that no man ever knew, save Duval, Lysette herself, and me. On the first night I came to Lysette's house, it was after a difficult day. Duval and I stayed as Lysette's guests long after the door had closed to the public, and I am ashamed to admit, became roaring drunk on her very good brandy. Our debauch resulted in a knife-throwing competition. The end result was that I put a blade right across the canvas of one of her favorite paintings—a Boucher." He grins. "Rather a lewd one, as I recall. Lysette never did forgive me for that. I suspect it was why she made me use the name as my password, a reminder at every opportunity of what my drunken escapade had cost her."

I find myself laughing out loud with him and Callie at the mental picture his words create.

"So—you were like the Scarlet Pimpernel," Callie says, a far away look, almost like longing, in her eyes. "Rescuing aristocrats from the revolution."

Guidry laughs. "Nothing is ever quite so clear as it is in the books. But, yes, we did our share. And Lysette—her house was the perfect cover, first in Paris, and later, in Spain. She was braver than us all. She, and her unusual friends." He smiles at Callie, whose eyes are glowing with something akin to hero worship.

"Unusual because they were like you?" I ask curiously.

"Some, perhaps." Guidry regards me through opaque eyes, and I get the feeling there is much he isn't saying. "Others were of your husband's kind. Still others were different again." His eyes return to Callie, whose face has fallen slightly. "You know," says Guidry slowly, his eyes resting on Callie's face, "when I was a young man, before my village was destroyed by the French, there was a place the men of my tribe went to speak to their ancestors. A clearing in the bayou—the same place, I believe, that your brother Connor was recently made wolf. My people went there to take *momoy*, jimson weed, to open their minds. Sometimes the ancestors spoke to them. Sometimes not. But such places hold power. Those who heard voices there, had visions, did not do so because the place alone was special. They did so because they were special enough to seek out those places." He smiles gently at Callie. "You are not here by chance, Callie. Some of the bravest of Madame Lysette's network were human—and no less extraordinary for being so." She smiles back at him, and again, I feel grateful for his kindness.

"Now!" He stands up in a fluid movement. "You can practice your accent, and your skills at war, and tell me the address again, *ma petite*."

"La Rue Vivienne, *en* Filles-Saint-Thomas," recites Callie obediently.

"And my password?"

"*Boucher*."

"Excellent." He winks at her. "You, my child, will make a superb spy. Anyway," he says, going to the door. "That is more than enough talk of the past. Let us enjoy what we may of the present, no?" Smiling at us, he goes out. It's only as he closes the door behind him that I realize I had, for a time at least, managed to forget about what lies ahead.

CHAPTER 7

PROTECTION

I wake the next morning more refreshed than I have been in days. Antoine is already down at the construction site, where work is underway despite the early hour. Iara knocks on the door after I've showered.

"I have come to look at you," she says, smiling tentatively and nodding at my belly. I nod for her to come in, and she asks me to lie down. Her hands move confidently over my belly, her face serious with concentration.

"Callie says you have a lot of experience as a midwife." I'm trying not to betray how nervous I feel. Iara nods.

"My mother brought many babies into the world. Everyone came to her. I was helping birth babies before I could speak." She steps back and smiles at me. "The babies have dropped. They are in a good position. Everything is as it should be. It's only a week until the equinox. You will meet your babies soon."

I struggle upright. "He seems very sure I will give birth on the equinox."

Iara smiles in understanding. "I know this is strange for you. For me, not so much. Katiusca feels the movement of earth and water. And you, especially, are connected to the tidal forces. The

57

babies will come at the equinox, as he says." She nods down toward the platform. "He has asked to speak with you today. Will you come with me?"

I haven't left the mansion in days. It feels good to have grass beneath my feet, inhale the rich scent of magnolias and river mud. Billowing clouds are bright white over the slow-moving water. Spring is normally a time of clear blue skies in Deepwater, but these clouds seem still and ominous, like a summer storm is building.

Antoine and Guidry are supervising work on the platform, Tate nowhere in sight. As we approach, Antoine is laughing aloud at something Guidry says, but he falls silent when he sees me, his eyes becoming dark and watchful. It hurts to see him withdraw. I know he wishes I would reconsider taking Katiusca's sacrifice. No matter which way I think on it, though, I don't see an alternative that will provide the same protection the shaman can. And Katiusca is willing. I am honest enough to admit that is no small part of my acceptance of his offer. I can't bear the thought of taking a life by force.

Katiusca comes toward us, chattering rapidly, his face creased in a smile. He squats down on the wooden boards as he talks, jabbing them with a stick to make his point.

"Katiusca says that he will begin to dance as dusk falls. I am not allowed on the platform while you are giving birth." A shadow of hurt crosses Iara's face. "I cannot dance for the kanobotuma. My transformation means the water no longer moves through me. I cannot raise the serpent nor help work the magic of our ancestors, but it is permitted for me to assist the birth." She listens to Katiusca. "He says he will dance throughout the birth. He will raise the serpent that will protect the land, and you, as the twins are born."

Antoine and Guidry are standing off to one side, listening. "Then it is Katiusca who will keep Keziah at bay?" Antoine asks. His tone is polite enough, but his eyes on Katiusca are steely.

"Yes—" Iara breaks off, frowning. She listens a little more to Katiusca then asks a question. His answer is swift and decisive. Iara asks another question, and this time Katiusca glares at her and his answer, when it comes, is rapid and holds a stern note of authority. Iara bows her head and turns back to Antoine, her eyes shifting uneasily. "Katiusca says that you, Antoine, and Cass must stand guard at the riverbank. You will be on this side, the wolves on the other."

"I will be with Harper." Antoine's answer is swift and decisive.

"Katiusca says no." Iara's eyes are on the shaman, so she doesn't see the sudden narrowing of Antoine's, the dangerous gleam in them as he stiffens.

"Then you will kindly explain to Katiusca that there are some things he cannot dictate. I will be at Harper's side until it is time for her to become vampire." Antoine's voice is flat, hard, and uncompromising.

"You don't understand." Iara looks at him. "It must be you and Cass here on the water. Only those connected to her by blood can protect Harper and the land that is hers. I will be concentrating on the birth. Katiusca needs you and Cass to hold the river, keep Keziah away. He says you must stop Keziah from putting foot on this soil until after Harper is turned. His protection is linked to the water. If Keziah crosses it before he binds himself to Harper, none of us will be safe."

Antoine's eyes are iron hard. Guidry is equally grim-faced when he asks, "What of the wolves?"

"Connor, Remy, and the pack will remain on the far bank and do what they can to stop Keziah from crossing." Iara glances at me. "Katiusca does not believe they can hold her long."

Guidry snorts. "Does he not, then."

"You won't be with them," Iara says, turning to Guidry.

His eyes narrow slightly. "Go on."

"You and Tate will guard the other approach to the mansion."

I brace for Guidry's explosion. He's not the kind of man to be relegated to the rear guard of a fight. And he certainly won't embrace the idea of being stationed with Tate. Guidry, however, surprises us all. He stares into the distance, as if making mental calculations, then his eyes snap back into focus and he nods curtly. "Makes sense."

Antoine stares at him. "No," he says flatly. "It does not, Guidry. I want you here, in case she gets over the river."

"If I'm with you and something comes from the other side, Harper and Iara will have only Takatoka for protection. It is not enough." His clinical assessment is a reminder of Guidry's many years at war.

"Harper will have me!" Antoine raises his voice, his eyes flashing angrily. He turns to Katiusca. "Tell him," he says tightly to Iara. "I don't care what excuses he makes. Nobody goes near Harper while our twins are being born unless I am there. I will be at her side throughout, until the moment I turn her and bind the sun into her body."

"When it is time for Harper to be turned, Katiusca says she must be brought to the platform, where it is safe and he can protect her. But until then you must be here, Antoine. Cass cannot hold the riverbank alone." Iara meets Antoine's eyes steadily. "The moment the twins are born, I will carry Harper to the platform, Antoine. She will be safe."

"And what of the twins?" My voice sounds rusty. Everyone turns to me. "You are all worried about what will happen to me," I say, unable to keep the anger from my voice. "But what happens to the twins while Iara is carrying me to the platform and Antoine is turning me? Who will protect them? If the platform is the safest place, then why am I not giving birth there?"

Iara translates and Katiusca bursts into a torrent of protest, gesticulating wildly. "He says the platform will be dangerous for you and your babies while he makes this magic." Iara shakes her head decisively. "You cannot be there while he raises the four-headed serpent." She looks at me. "Katiusca will be dancing your death, and his," she says quietly. "Your transformation into vampire, the joining of your spirits. He is calling up forces that will make you strong enough to fight Keziah. Such magic is no place for your babies." She looks at Antoine. "And you must be here, waiting," she says. "When it is time to make Harper, she will need you to be ready."

"No harm will come to your young," Guidry rasps. His eyes are gray and steady on Antoine's. "I may not love your brother. But I've witnessed his fighting prowess firsthand. He and I will keep them safe, friend." He clasps Antoine's shoulder. "If I must lose my own life to do it, I swear I will keep them safe."

"Jeremiah and I will stay with Harper, too." I hadn't realized Callie was there until she pipes up, her pointed face resolute. "I know you think we're just humans and can't help. But we've both fought before. I won't leave Harper's side, Antoine. I promise."

To my surprise, it's Guidry who answers her. "I've no doubt," he says gruffly. His hand touches her shoulder. "You are a brave one, child." He meets Antoine's skeptical eyes steadily. "Let your friends help. You are the one Keziah fears the most. The best place for you is holding her away, until your young are born safe."

Antoine stares hard at him. Guidry holds his eyes just as resolutely. Finally, Antoine clicks his tongue with an impatient sound and looks away. I take his hand. It is unyielding at first, then his fingers curl around my own, so tightly they hurt. He looks down at me.

"We have to trust them, Antoine."

His mouth tightens. He nods curtly. Though he doesn't speak, I know exactly what he is thinking, because the same words are going through my head: *it's not like we have a choice.*

CHAPTER 8

THREE

Connor and the pack arrive soon after we finish speaking. Antoine and Guidry immediately begin explaining what Katiusca said, and they walk together up to the mansion, deep in conversation about strategy. I watch them go with an inward sigh of relief. "Callie." I smile at her. "Would you mind fetching me some juice?"

"On it." Beaming at me, she takes off up the slope. I happen to know the juice is out, so I figure I've bought myself a little time. I turn to Iara.

"I have some questions for Katiusca. Can you translate?" Iara nods and the two of them settle themselves cross-legged on the floorboards. I'm sitting on an upturned crate. In the center of the platform lies the long canvas bag Katiusca brought with him from Venezuela. It's still tied shut. Antoine told me Katiusca never leaves it, even sleeping here at night.

"The kanobotuma are inside," Iara explains as she follows my gaze. Her language is much more fluent today, as it always is when she is well rested. "When Katiusca is ready to begin his dance, he will bring them out and nail them to the posts on each corner. He says that until then, they must be kept hidden, away from curious eyes."

It's midmorning, the air fresh and clear, but something about that bag makes the atmosphere on the platform feel thick and still. All around the garden, birds call from tree branches. I notice that none perch on the wooden frame under which we sit, though.

"Katiusca has spoken a lot about what will happen while I give birth." I wait while Iara translates. "But he hasn't said anything about how we will defeat Keziah afterward. Apart from showing me the zemi of Guabancex, and saying it is the key to Keziah's destruction, I know nothing of what I need to do to kill her." I look between them. "If the Abatey is inside me, and Katiusca will become part of me, then I'm the one who has to kill her. Aren't I?"

Iara stares at me. I can't tell if it's pity or fear I see in her eyes. Maybe both, I think. She turns to Katiusca and they talk quickly. His eyes, which have rested on me throughout the discussion, slip away so I can't read them. He speaks rapidly and with authority to Iara, whose face colors. I watch her closely. Perhaps I'm projecting my own fears, but Iara seems as uneasy as I feel.

"What is he saying, Iara?"

She inhales sharply and turns to me, biting her lip as if considering her words carefully. "You must understand that Katiusca is the wisest shaman of my people." Her eyes slide away from mine. "Much of what he knows cannot be explained, even to me. I can tell you some things. Others you will only understand after his spirit is joined with yours."

I try not to let my face show the instinctual recoil I feel whenever I contemplate the process of allowing Katiusca access to my body, my spirit, my soul.

"Katiusca says that after you are drained, and then given the blood of immortality, he will come to you here, on this platform. You will take his life as the sun rises and is bound to your body. All this will take place under the protection of the serpent's magic he will dance into being. So long as he lives, Keziah will not be able to reach you through the magic he weaves. But the moment Katiusca leaves his body and his spirit comes alive in you, his protection will be broken. Keziah will be able to cross onto this land and reach you. That is when you will confront her."

"What about the others?" I say. "The wolves, Antoine and Cass? Keziah has run from them before. Why does he think she will not run this time?"

"Katiusca says Keziah will not come here alone. She will have others with her."

"Others?" I frown. "Does he have proof of this? Has he told Antoine? Tate?"

"They are suspecting, anyway," Iara says quietly. "It makes sense, Harper. Keziah knows the kind of force we have. She will prepare for it."

"Okay." I digest this. "So she'll come with an army, and Katiusca believes she will break through our defenses. Which brings it back to me. How am I supposed to defeat her?" My stomach churns uneasily, as it does every time I contemplate facing Keziah. And not only because I fear her. Because I don't know what I will be when I face her. If I'm honest with myself, that unknown is what frightens me, more than anything else.

"When Katiusca becomes one with you, his knowledge will be yours." Iara looks at me gravely. "He says: Do not fear. You will know how to call Guabancex and use her power, in a way Keziah does not once you have the power of the wisiratu. Katiusca will guide you from within."

I can't suppress a slight shudder at even the idea of this. Iara smiles reassuringly. "Do not be afraid, Harper. There are things you cannot yet know. Katiusca says that you must trust him. After your transformation you will know what to do."

Iara no doubt intends to comfort me. But despite her reassurances, I sense a shadow behind her eyes and have an uneasy feeling that there is something she isn't telling me.

"Where will you be while I'm being transformed?"

"I will not leave you during the birth. The moment the twins are born, I will carry you from the mansion to the platform here." Iara's eyes don't waver on mine, though again, I sense something shifting behind them.

"And the twins?"

"Tate, Guidry, Callie, and Jeremiah will all be with them. And I will return to them as soon as I have brought you to the platform." *There,* I think with an odd jolt. *That's where it is, whatever it is she won't tell me. Something happens when she brings me here.*

"Do you promise me?" I hold her eyes. "You promise me on your life that my twins will be kept safe, no matter what happens?"

"I promise, Harper." This time there is no flicker in her eyes. "I give you my word, on my life, that your children will be safe. All of us will see to it."

"You know how they travel." My chest clenches. "They need to wear the pendants from the moment they are born, Iara, or they may go somewhere and not be able to return. Will you make certain they have them before you take me from the room?"

"Of course." Iara takes my hand. "Do not worry for your children, Harper. We will protect them."

I walk slowly toward the mansion, unable to shake my unease. *What are they planning?* I go over Iara's words in my mind, trying to work out what it is that I'm missing. Just below the porch, it hits me.

There are three shamans.

The Warao always have three shamans: the bahanarotu, the hoarotu, and the wisiratu. Keziah herself was one of three, but now she is just one, alone.

Iara is the daughter of a union between a wisiratu and hoarotu. She holds, too, the spirit of the bahanarotu she drank. She possesses all three shamans in her blood, yes—but she does not have the knowledge to wield the magic she holds. Her companion spirit is the bahanarotu, not the wisiratu. She does not have the ability to summon ancestral magic, to bind the three into one.

But the wisiratu, I think, the hairs standing up on the back of my neck, cannot summon that magic without the power of the other two. Katiusca cannot summon Guabancex alone. And the only way it is possible for him to gain access to the power he needs is if it flows in my blood.

There is a reason Katiusca doesn't want Antoine anywhere near me before my transformation, and it has nothing to do with fighting off Keziah.

He never intended Antoine to be the one to turn me.

He means for Iara to do it.

Only Iara's blood contains the power of the three Warao shamans, the power Katiusca knows we will need if I am to summon Guabancex and defeat Keziah.

I stare at the open door to the mansion, hearing the low rumble of Antoine's voice within, and I know two things with absolute certainty.

One is that Antoine will never agree to Katiusca's plan.

And the second is that he won't have to, because I will never tell him.

CHAPTER 9

NAMES

Jeremiah arrives five days before the equinox.

I'm in the kitchen with Callie when his motorcycle pulls up outside. She goes very still. Her eyes travel to me, as if she's waiting for something.

"Go." I smile at her. A moment later she's out on the porch, at the top of the stairs. Jeremiah climbs off the bike. He may not be any taller than when he left, but he's filled out plenty. His face is watchful and intelligent. I have the impression that somewhere in his months away the boy who grew up poverty stricken in a trailer has collided with the man who knows his own worth, and with it, what he wants. His eyes settle on the figure on the porch.

"Callie." He says the name like he's coming home.

"Jeremiah." Her voice is higher than normal, without any of the usual accent she adopts when nervous. He takes the steps slowly, his eyes never leaving her, until he's standing barely inches away. He reaches behind him and draws a long, slim case from his back. It looks just like Callie's own. "I trained with the sword you gave me as a going away present," he says, holding it out to her. "Every morning. Just like you taught me."

"Oh." I can't see Callie's face. "So I guess you think you can beat me now, huh." The words may be bold, but her tone holds none of her customary bravado.

"No." Jeremiah gives her a small smile. "I don't." Reaching down, he takes her hand. "But I was hoping you might give me a chance to at least try, while I'm here."

Callie is staring down at her hand in his. "I thought you might be too busy," she says, her voice a little muffled.

"Well, you thought wrong. Callie," Jeremiah says quietly, "why haven't you answered my calls?"

I ease myself away from the door. This doesn't feel like a conversation I should be part of. I head for the back porch just in time to hear Callie say, her voice half a sob, "I didn't want to bug you. I figured you needed your space."

I don't need to stay to know that Jeremiah is about to tell her that space is the last thing he needs. I head out back, looking down the slope to where Antoine is straddling the frame of the pagoda, banging something into place. A bittersweet pain clenches my heart as I watch him. It seems a hard irony, that just as Callie and Jeremiah seem finally to have discovered the truth in how they feel about one another, I must live a lie.

I sit on the swing seat. A breeze blows hair across my face, and the babies stir inside me. I put one hand on my belly and with the other clasp the pendants at my throat. "I wish you could take me away," I whisper, looking down at the mound of my belly. "I wish you could take Antoine and me both away, to another time, another place, where none of this danger exists. I wish I could have you just like any other woman has children. Just be your mother. Nothing else. Not a vampire, or an Abatey. Just the mother who gives you life." The twins move slowly under my hand, as if they hear me. The breeze stirs the air around me with more force. "Is that you, Tessa?" I look around. The leaves of the moon vine are shivering on the columns. The red magnolia by the porch is leaning as if in a strong wind, while down at the river, the water is still, the trees hanging over it unmoving. "I know you're here," I whisper. "I wish you could tell me what to do, Tessa. I want Antoine to be the one to change me, more than anything. But if he does, what if I don't have the strength to defend our girls? I want to tell him the truth. But I know that if I do, he will never leave my side. He'll never allow Katiusca to control how I am made. And what if that costs me my girls' lives? How am I supposed to live with that?"

A gust of wind tosses petals from the red magnolia across my face. They stroke my cheek as they fall to my lap. Tears fill my eyes. "I know you said you would always be here," I whisper. "And you are. But just this once, Tessa, I wish you could talk back, tell me what to do. Because I don't know. I truly don't know."

"What is it you don't know?" I spin my head to find Guidry looking at me curiously from the end of the porch. "I've seen people speak to their unborn young before." He grins at me. "Normally it's nonsense, though. You sounded like you were expecting an answer of some kind."

"I wish." I half smile at him. "Where did you spring from?"

"The two on the front porch didn't much seem like they wanted company. Thought it best to come around the side."

"That's Jeremiah," I begin.

"I know who he is." Guidry settles himself on the bench near my swing seat. "You called one of your babes Tessa." He glances at me. "That one of the names you're going to choose?"

"It was my sister's name."

"Was?"

"She's gone now." Guidry nods. I like that about him, that he doesn't need a lot of explanation. "I want to call one of the twins Marguerite, after Antoine's sister."

"Well, that's something." Guidry tilts his head, nodding slowly. His face has gone oddly pale, but when he catches me looking more closely at him, he smiles, and I think it might have been a trick of the light.

"Yes. Marguerite is a lovely name. And Antoine would like that, I think." His smile fades, lips thinning into a hard line. He clears his throat. "Takatoka too, I imagine." I look at him in surprise and he makes a rough sound in his throat. "Don't like the man," he says. "Never will. But he did love that girl, that I do know."

"Yes." Tate had been destined to marry Marguerite, until Antoine made him a vampire. Tate has always thought Antoine turned him primarily to ensure that Marguerite would make a socially acceptable marriage that would enable her to inherit the mansion and pass on the Marigny name, thus keeping the binding that held Keziah and Caleb intact. He believes, too, that it was done in a rage of bloodlust and anger at Tate himself, who had forced Antoine to become a vampire so Marguerite could be spared.

I know that Antoine was driven by something greater than either of those things—that he couldn't bear the thought of living out immortality alone, without the man he considered the brother of his heart, if not by blood. They may have been estranged for much of the intervening centuries, and Tate may still not be aware of the true reason behind Antoine turning him, but I know how tightly bound Antoine and Tate remain, not least through their shared love for Marguerite. Both of them, in their own way, gave their lives for her. Naming one of the twins for her seems a fitting way to honor both their sacrifices, and Marguerite's.

"The other name, I'm not sure of yet," I tell him.

"What does Antoine think?"

I look down at where Antoine is still working on the roof. We'd agreed on the name Marguerite long ago. We'd considered Tessa for the other, but it doesn't feel right to me. Tessa is still here, all around me. I can't imagine giving her name to another.

And since my decision to accept Katiusca as my companion spirit, Antoine and I have had trouble talking about the weather, let alone baby names. "I don't know what Antoine thinks," I say quietly.

"Would you allow me to make a suggestion?" I turn to Guidry in surprise. He's looking down toward the river, his fingers slowly tearing apart an oak leaf. He catches my look and his mouth twists. "Not about names," he clarifies. "Such things are not my place. I mean about Antoine."

I raise my eyebrows and wait.

"Sometimes there are things that are best kept secret. Even from those we love. No matter how difficult it is to stay silent." He stares fixedly down at the river, and I get the feeling he is speaking with great care. "Whatever you decide to do in order to protect your children," he says quietly, "trust your instincts, Harper. Even if it means you don't entirely tell the truth."

I'm so taken aback it's hard to think straight. "That seems like odd advice," I say finally, staring at his profile, "from Antoine's oldest friend."

When he turns sharply to face me, his eyes gleam with a hard, dangerous topaz light. "It's good advice," he says in the savage growl he rarely displays in front of me, "from someone who, if you will forgive me, knows your husband better than anyone. And who wants to make sure he doesn't lose those he loves the most."

"Like you did," I say quietly. "I am so sorry for what happened to your family, Guidry."

He stands abruptly and turns away so that when he speaks, I can't read his face.

"Losing my wife and children was a tragedy. One it took many years to recover from." His shoulders lift as he breathes deeply, as if bracing himself to say his next words. "Many years later, though, I lost someone else. A woman I loved just as much as I had my wife. More, perhaps, for by then I was a man full-grown who knew what a risk it was, to love in such a way." I remain silent, unwilling to interrupt such an intimate confession. "She, too, kept secrets to protect those she loved. She kept them from me, knowing I would never have agreed. And at first, I couldn't forgive her that." His head drops. A moment later when he turns back to face me, his eyes are dark and fathomless with old pain, his voice rasping like old metal. "In time, though, I saw her decision for what it was: unimaginably brave. Heroic, even. And I realized that sometimes, the hardest, and bravest, thing we can do is sacrifice truth for the right outcome. So I do understand, Harper. Better than you might think. But even more than that, I understand the pain of losing those you love more than anything in this world."

He looks over my shoulder, into the distant past. "In the beginning," he says quietly, "after she was—gone, I was nearly mad with grief, and anger. Antoine never left my side. Not for months, years even. Not until I could bear to live a day without throwing myself at the nearest battlefield—or bottle—I could find." His eyes rest on mine, burning with the intensity I always sense in him, simmering just beneath the cynical exterior. "I would not see Antoine endure such agony, after all this time. I would do anything to spare him that, even if it means keeping secrets."

His gaze moves from me, traveling restlessly over the water below. "Antoine and Takatoka are close," he says curtly, clearly not wanting a response. "I will leave you. I'm sure you have a great deal to think about."

He leaps from the porch without another word. A moment later, he is gone, no more than a shadow between the trees, then nothing at all.

∼

I'M STILL SITTING ON THE PORCH AS TATE AND ANTOINE LAND ON our side of the river. Tate comes up the slope first, leaving Antoine down by the pagoda.

"You look very thoughtful." He settles himself in the seat recently occupied by Guidry. His gentle smile and direct look could not be more of a contrast from the savage edge to the wolf who just left.

"I was just thinking of names. For the twins."

"Oh?" He raises his eyebrows politely.

"Yes." I give him a tentative smile. "Antoine and I thought—that is, I wanted—we both did." I stop, gathering myself. "I'm not doing this very well. We wanted to name one of the girls after Marguerite." I meet his eyes. "Are you—would it upset you, if we did that?"

Tate pales as I speak, but by the time I'm finished, his face has regained color, and the dark shadows in his eyes have cleared. "I think that Marguerite would be honored." Reaching out, he touches my hand briefly with his own. "It is thoughtful of you to consider me. Please allow me to say that I can't imagine a better way to remember her. For what it is worth, Harper, you have my blessing."

"Thankyou." I grip his hand gratefully. We sit in silence for a time.

"Do you have a second name?" he asks finally.

"Not yet." I explain that I don't feel comfortable naming one of my daughters after Tessa. "But I can't think of anything else that fits, really."

"I'm sure the right name will come to you." He smiles and stands as Antoine comes toward us. "And that it will be perfect when it does." Touching my shoulder, he goes indoors.

"What's perfect?" Antoine has come up the slope as we've been talking. He takes the steps in one easy lope and sprawls on the swing seat, one arm behind me, his eyes gleaming cobalt and gold as he smiles, covering my hand with his own. "Oof! They are dancing today, aren't they?"

"I'm still trying to come up with another name," I say cautiously. It's the most relaxed I've seen Antoine in days, and I'm not entirely certain what has wrought the change. "Tate gave us his blessing to use Marguerite for one of the girls."

"I'm glad." Antoine nods, one of his thumbs stroking my shoulder. He draws a breath as if he's going to speak, then doesn't.

"What is it?"

He tilts his head and rubs one hand over his jaw. "We're naming one of the girls after my sister. I think the other name should come from your family."

"There is one name." I glance sideways at him. "It was my grandmother's name, on my mother's side. I don't remember her very well, but I know Mom adored her, and always said that Tessa and I looked just like her. She was European, or her parents were. They came to America when she was very young, I think." I frown, feeling a familiar ache at all the questions I can never ask anyone now. "I don't know much about our family history. Anyway." I smile at Antoine, who is watching me with the quiet cobalt stare that makes me feel heard and understood. "I don't want to name one of our girls after Mom, or Tessa. It feels too recent. But I do want to hand down something of our legacy, I guess. And I've always loved the name." I hold his eyes. "Aurelia. It means *the golden one*."

"Aurelia." He tries the name on his tongue. "I like that. Oh!" Antoine's eyes widen as he stares down in fascination at where his hand still rests on my belly. "It seems one of the babies likes that name too," he says, grinning. "That was a mighty kick she just gave. Do you think she heard us?"

"Definitely." I hold my belly, feeling the two little bodies stir beneath it. "Aurelia and Marguerite," I say softly. "I think they are perfect."

"*The golden one* and *the pearl*," Antoine says. He smiles crookedly at me. "Aurelia, the golden one, and Marguerite, the pearl."

"Do you like them?"

"I love them." His eyes hold mine as his smile fades. "I'm sorry, Harper," he says quietly.

"For what?"

"You know for what." His lips touch mine in a long, quiet kiss, one that says all that I need to know. "I was afraid," he says when he pulls away. "I still am. I don't trust that little shaman. Even if I do think he can help protect us, the thought of him becoming a part of you terrifies me." He takes my hand in his, stroking it with his thumb. "But the reality is that I'd be terrified no matter who you took as your companion spirit. The thought of anyone changing you, of you being anything other than the Harper I spoke to on the jetty that first day we met, chills me to the bone." He looks down at our joined hands, then back at me. "But the reality is, you've already changed. You changed when the Abatey inside you was activated, and you found the courage to make the potion that transformed Connor—just as you found the courage to save me by giving me your own blood. You were brave long before we ever met: you gave your kidney to Tessa to try to save her, and you survived the death of your mother." His hand on mine is warm and steady. "I think of you as human. Young and frail. But the truth, Harper, is that you'd already endured a lifetime of pain before we ever met. And now, somehow, you're carrying miracle twins able to travel through time." He laughs softly and kisses the top of my head. "If there's anyone who will know the right thing to do, it's you. And besides—it is me who will turn you into a vampire. No matter who becomes your companion spirit, you and I will be bound forever, Harper. I can live with that."

I'm glad his head is resting on mine, so he can't see my face. Guilt tears my chest so I can't speak. I feel like a traitor even sitting there, and suddenly I know that regardless of Guidry's advice, I can't do this, deceive him this way.

I have opened my mouth to tell him the truth when Jeremiah comes out onto the porch, Callie just behind him. "Antoine." He puts out his hand, smiling slowly. Antoine stands and takes the outstretched hand, looking Jeremiah up and down with curious eyes. There's something in the handshake that is an acceptance of the man Jeremiah has become these past months, an acknowledgment that they are no longer guardian and boy—but men, together.

"Well," says Antoine, glancing at Callie's flushed face then back at Jeremiah, nodding slowly. "Well, then. Welcome home, Jeremiah."

I watch them from the swing seat, feeling my secret sink back inside me, away from the surface.

CHAPTER 10

FAMILY

Avery and Remy arrive late in the afternoon. Hair still wet from the shower, holding hands, and barely able to look at anyone else, they're both clearly delirious with happiness at being back together again. Iara, Callie, Cass, and I have been cooking all afternoon, or rather, I've been sitting at the table watching while they do the work. Remy goes to join the party down back, and Avery stays with us. The platform is in place, the roof nearly finished. I'm not certain how I feel about that. The phrase "final nail in the coffin" echoes in my head every time I look at it. When that pagoda is finished, it will be time for my human life to end also.

It doesn't get any easier to think of.

The words I wanted to say to Antoine have disappeared inside me again, into the ongoing argument my head and heart are having. My head insists that doing what I know will best keep the twins safe is the smart option. My head understands exactly why Katiusca and Iara have kept their plans a secret. Like me, they know what Antoine will say and do if he learns it is Iara, and not him, that they intend to be my Maker.

But my heart screams that concealing the truth from

Antoine is the worst of all betrayals, one he may never find it in himself to forgive, no matter how long immortality grants us together. My heart asks how I would feel if the situation was reversed. Possibly hardest of all, my heart breaks at the thought that I will be bound, for all eternity, not to the man I love and to whom I have sworn my life, but to Iara, purely because her blood can grant me the power to destroy Keziah.

That final thought brings me back around to the arguments of my head: unless I destroy Keziah, none of us, including Antione and our daughters, will ever be safe. It is the closing of that circle that silences me when I would tell Antoine the truth.

"Penny for your thoughts." Avery smiles as she sits on the chair beside me.

"You look happy." I return her smile. "I'm so glad you and Remy are managing to make it work long-distance."

"It isn't easy. I really miss him. But it's still easier to be at college and know we're together, than away and wondering how he feels." She laughs a little. "Remy came up to see me, you know. At college."

"He did?" The thought of Remy, with his cutoff twill shirts and burly muscles, mingling with clean-cut college boys, seems quite improbable. "How did that go?"

"It was hard at first, for him more than me. But then we went to a party. Remy put down a gallon of beer in one long swig and managed to fix one of the guy's trucks. After that it seemed to go okay," she says as I start laughing. "And his visit had the added bonus of scaring the rest of campus off enough that I could finally go to the gym in peace, which, believe me, was a relief—and not only for me. Poor Jeremiah had been doing overtime on big brother duty."

Callie looks up sharply at that, and I wince inwardly. Avery can be truly tactless at times.

"This is about ready," Cass says, meeting my eyes and subtly rolling her own. I'm clearly not the only one to notice Callie's reaction. "Callie, would you go down and let Jeremiah and the others know we're ready to eat, if they want to wash up?" Callie leaves the kitchen quietly, her face closed. Iara is out back laying places on the trestle tables that we've taken to eating at, since we've found ourselves feeding a small army on a daily basis.

"Avery." Cass waits until Callie is well out of earshot before she folds her arms and fixes Avery with a hard stare. "Do you have one ounce of sense in that beautiful head of yours?"

"What?" Avery looks between us, her sheet of rich black hair hanging straight to her slender waist, perfect almond eyes wide and innocent. Avery's saving grace has always been that underneath the exquisite beauty on the surface, she has a truly good heart. Even that, however, doesn't seem to give her the ability to read a room. She is one of the least emotionally perceptive people I know.

"Callie has spent the past eight months wondering how Jeremiah feels about her," Cass says, "or if he even thinks of her at all. When the two of you headed off to college together she was terrified that he would fall more in love with you than he already was. And now, just when it looks like she and Jeremiah might actually have a chance, you make it sound as though he's been nothing more than your lapdog for that entire time, chasing off all the other men who want to date you. Didn't you see her face?"

"But that's ridiculous." Avery looks bewildered. "Jeremiah and I are just friends, nothing more. What?" she says, looking between Cass and me. "What am I supposed to do? Tell her Jeremiah has eyes only for her?"

"Try to think of something," I say. "Surely you can see how little confidence she has."

"Fine." Avery rolls her eyes and stomps off outside.

"The more things change, huh?" Cass shoots me a wry grin that quickly fades to an expression of concern. "Are you okay, Harper?" She grimaces. "I mean, apart from the whole having-time-traveling babies, becoming-a-vampire thing." We look at each other and burst out laughing. If there's one person who really does understand what I'm going through, it's Cass. In the past year, she's not only been forcibly turned into a vampire and seen her mother murdered in front of her by Keziah, but also had to learn to live with my brother becoming a werewolf in order to save her from Keziah's mind control. I'm not the only one whose life Keziah has turned upside down. That fact slips onto the invisible seesaw in my mind—on one end of which sits the arguments of my head, while on the other, my heart. This falls on the head side, yet another piece that weighs it down. The heart side is light indeed, carrying only my own selfish desires. They do not feel to me like any balance to the heavy weight of considerations on the other end: the possible destruction Keziah may still wield on all those I love.

"Harper." Cass's concern is palpable, and I realize my thoughts must be all over my face. "You know you can talk to me."

"I know." I force a smile. "I'm just not sure that talking is going to help, Cass."

"Try me." She takes my hand, and I cover it with my own.

"Maybe later." I struggle to my feet. "Let's go and eat." I can feel her eyes on my back, but I'm not ready to talk about my internal seesaw. Not even to Cass.

THE SHADOWS GROW LONG AS WE SIT AT TRESTLE TABLES WEIGHED down beneath Iara's paella, Cass's gumbo, a mountain of salads, and the steaks Connor has grilled. Guidry and Antoine sit together down one end of the table, Tate and Iara at another. Connor lands on the chair next to me, Cass opposite, Iara on my other side. Candles flicker in old bottles. Callie, knowing it makes me happy, has put bowls of flowers in among the food.

She sits opposite Jeremiah, who, I notice, never misses an opportunity to fill her glass or pass her food. He talks solely to her, turning away from any other conversation, and gradually I see her face soften again. I breathe a sigh of relief. I want very much for Callie and Jeremiah to be happy, whether as friends or more than that. They have both, in their own ways, lived such difficult lives, been very alone.

"Penny for your thoughts." Connor nudges me and I smile.

"You're the second person to say that to me tonight."

"Well, you do look deep in thought."

"I guess I was just thinking that everyone here has been through so much." I nod at Jeremiah and Callie. "Those two, for example. Do you realize they're the only completely normal humans left at our table? Even Avery has her supernatural ability to see and hear spirits. But Callie and Jeremiah have just had to learn to live with all this, without any powers to help them survive it."

"It looks like Jeremiah has been making up for that in the gym. He's twice the size he was when he left." Connor gestures at the uneaten steak on my plate. "You gonna eat that?"

I push the plate toward him. "Go ahead." He tears into it like a starving man, despite the two he's already devoured. I watch him with some amusement.

"I know, I know," he says, around a mouthful of meat. "Cass says I will need to take another job just to pay our grocery bill lately." He grins at me. "Go on, then. What's worrying you about Callie and Jeremiah? I thought they were pretty good with supernatural."

"They are. Clearly." I gesture at the table, rolling my eyes. "But you know what I mean. You and Cass—you've gone through so much to be together. Remy and the pack have had to come to terms not only with being wolves, but now with being immortal, as well. As for Antoine, and Tate, and Guidry—

between them, they've lived generations of heartbreak and difficulty."

"What's your point?"

"Well, Callie and Jeremiah have just had to—adjust. In their own way, they're even more alone than any of us. They're basically normal humans, caught up in a crazy, magical world. How are they ever supposed to just fit in with the world around them? I mean, Jeremiah has been off at college for months, but I can't imagine him ever bringing friends home to meet the family. It would take all of a matter of minutes for them to get the weird vibe."

Connor twists his head up to look at me with an expression of mock hurt. "Are you saying we're weird, Harper?" he says in an injured tone. "I'm wounded."

"Shut up, idiot." I swat him affectionately over the head. "You know what I mean."

"Oh, I don't know." Reaching for more potatoes, he casts a surreptitious look around the table. "I'd say this is actually a highly typical family environment." He tilts his head toward Guidry, then at Tate. "You've got the two brothers who hate each other—well, they may as well be brothers," he forestalls me. Nodding at Iara, next to me, he whispers, "The hot auntie who all the boys can't take their eyes off of. Come on," he says, laughing at my prim face, "even Jeremiah can't help staring when she walks out in shorts. She's ridiculously stunning, even for a vamp." I shrug. I can't argue with that.

He points his knife at Remy, who is currently feeding Avery from his own fork in a way that should probably come with a mature adult warning. "You've got the wild cousins, who definitely have a bottle of moonshine under the table, plus whatever illegal substances Remy has in the car. Wild cousins who, for the record, I will never—emphasis on the never—trust anywhere near my innocent little nieces." He pats my belly perfunctorily and puts his head close to it. "Did you hear your uncle Connor? Don't even think about going anywhere near that bayou, or I will be coming after you with fangs bared, little ones."

I'm trying not to draw any attention to us by giggling, but it's hard, especially when Remy raises his glass in open acknowledgment of Connor's insult and without losing a beat, goes back to feeding Avery.

Turning to the end of the table, Connor raises an eyebrow in Antoine's direction, his expression dry. "Then there is God himself, the almighty head of the household. Yes, I know, he's perfect," he waves me away, smiling to take the sting out of his words. "But in this scenario I'm the father of the bride who doesn't really like being displaced. Brother. Whatever. You know what I mean. Anyway." He blows a kiss to Cass across the table, who shakes her head at the two of us, clearly having overheard more than a little of our conversation. "The most beautiful girl in the world." He grins and winks at me. "And that is all I will say on Cass, for fear of my own safety. Perfection, darling," he says, when Cass rolls her eyes. "Utter perfection." She throws a bread roll across the table at him. "And so mature," he adds, blowing her another kiss.

"Finally," he says, "who could forget the eccentric great uncle, who everyone knows is quite mad?" He gestures to where Katiusca is sitting alone, down on the platform, away from us all.

I try to maintain my humor, but despite myself, my face must reveal something, because Connor's own smile fades. "Are you okay, Harper? Are you worried about the little shaman?"

"No." I try to smile. "Not worried, exactly. It's just that he's —" I glance up the table, relieved to find Antoine deep in conversation with Guidry and clearly not listening to ours. I put my mouth close to Connor's ear and barely breathe the words: "Katiusca's going to be the sacrifice."

Connor rears back, his eyes searching my face, flickering

down to the cross-legged figure, then back to me. He tilts his head slightly toward Antoine. "He knows this?"

I nod.

"And he's okay with it?"

I shake my head. Without warning, tears fill my eyes, and I look hastily down at my plate, pushing salad around with a fork.

Connor takes my hand underneath the table. "Are *you* okay with it?" he asks quietly, staring at his own plate so as not to draw unwanted attention.

I shake my head, then shrug, not knowing how to answer. Connor nods slowly. Putting his arm around me, he draws my head gently down to his shoulder and leaves his hand on my neck, calm and steady, a reassuring weight that says everything we can't. I rest there quietly for the rest of the meal, as the chatter of our family weaves around us.

MUCH LATER, AFTER DESSERT HAS BEEN AND GONE AND CONNOR and Cass have stood up to clear the dishes, Antoine takes my brother's place beside me.

"You and Connor seemed deep in conversation."

"You and Guidry, too." I turn the comment back on him.

He leans his head to gently touch his cheek to my hair in acknowledgment and raises it again. "Guidry told me I should trust you to do what is right for our twins."

I nod. "He said something similar to me."

"Really?" Antoine glances at me in surprise.

"We were talking about his past, about a woman he loved, a long time ago." I smile. "He said you were a good friend to him, after she was gone. I think he is just trying to protect you."

"He told you about his past? That is unlike him."

"He told me a little. Not much." I'm more interested in what

Antoine's reaction to his advice had been. "What did you say, when he told you to trust me?"

His eyes darken. "I asked him if he had found it easy, all those years ago, to let the woman he loved make dangerous decisions."

I try and fail not to wince.

Seeing my reaction, Antoine grimaces. "I was angry. I shouldn't have said it, or not publicly. There are some things that should never be brought up, especially at a dinner table. I'm fortunate Guidry knows me as he does. He let it go."

"She died, then? The woman Guidry loved? What was her name?"

"He never told me." Antoine's face is thoughtful. "Her identity was a closely guarded secret—I assumed it was because she was a double agent. I know only that she was lost in the Napoleonic wars, during a dangerous mission in which Guidry and I very nearly lost our own lives." He shakes his head. "All he would ever say about it was that it was her choice to sacrifice herself, a choice he had to respect. And he only revealed so much once, when he was very drunk." He lifts his shoulders slightly. "Some things are too painful to speak of, I guess. I never raised it with him again." He rubs his face wearily. "Until tonight. I shouldn't have said it," he repeats, shaking his head.

"Was he angry?"

"No." Antoine frowns. "He was just—quiet. He said that if we love someone, we have to let them make the decisions that are right for them, no matter how dangerous they might seem." He turns dark eyes to me.

"Harper." He puts his face close to mine so that amid the chatter, no one can hear us. "Do you wish to speak to me? Away from all this?" He flicks his eyes down the slope, where Katiusca, though now chatting away to Iara, who has brought him a plate of food, watches us through dark eyes.

For a moment, the temptation to tell him the whole truth is

almost overwhelming. It takes all my willpower to push it aside, but I do, not least because even if I thought that telling him was the right thing to do, now is not the time for it.

"No." I put my hand over Antoine's and smile. "Let's just enjoy tonight, shall we?" I leave the rest of my thought—that it might be the last time we have a chance to do so—unspoken.

~

THE NIGHT CARRIES ON, MOVING TO CHEESE AND BRANDY AND whatever Remy has in his clear glass jar. I leave the party at the table to go inside, waving away half a dozen offers of help. It's only when I enter the mansion that I realize Callie and Avery are talking, just outside the entrance to the bathroom. "You have to understand," Avery is saying, "why Jeremiah and I wound up being so close." I come to a halt, staying in the shadows, uncomfortable eavesdropping, but equally uncomfortable with the idea of allowing Callie to be hurt, and poised to intervene if necessary.

"It's really none of my business." Callie goes to walk away, and Avery grabs her arm.

"No, Callie, wait. Please let me explain." Callie comes to a reluctant stop. "Jeremiah and I both tried to date at first. Other people," Avery adds hastily, seeing Callie's face.

"I thought you were with Remy when you left? I saw the two of you get back together at the wedding." Since their reconciliation had, unbeknownst to Avery, been of Callie's doing, this is something of an understatement.

"We did. But then Remy spoke to Guidry, and he learned about the whole immortality thing. It threw us both, I guess. He wanted me to date other people, and if I'm being honest, I wondered if I might not be better off with someone else, too. A normal life, so to speak." She makes air quotes with her fingers. "I tried to date. I did. But then one of the guys tried to kiss me, and I just couldn't do it. Jeremiah found me crying on a bench outside the dorm, too embarrassed to go inside. He was kind to me, like always. He listened."

I can feel Callie's hurt, and I'm still ready to step in, unsure where this is going.

"But don't get the wrong idea." Avery touches Callie's arm. "He told me one bad date shouldn't put me off forever, and that I should give dating another go. I told Jeremiah that I would if he did. So we shook on it, and he set me up with a friend of his. I did the same for him."

"What happened?" Callie asks, and although I know I should leave now, knowing she's okay, I can't bring myself to. I want to hear the end of this too.

"My night was a disaster. The guy was nice enough, but he liked French films and nice wine. All I wanted was to be in the bayou, hanging my legs off the jetty, drinking a cold beer and listening to the pack play guitar." Callie laughs aloud at that, and I smile too. For all her stunning looks, Avery is a Deepwater girl, born and bred. "But Jeremiah's date was even worse." Avery smiles at Callie. "I didn't see Jeremiah that night, or the next day. I asked my friend how it went, and she said she thought Jeremiah was the nicest guy she'd ever met, and she was really hoping he'd call her—but that she was worried he was hung up on his ex. I couldn't work out who she was talking about, until she asked me if I knew someone named Callie."

I bite my lip, tears pricking my eyes.

"I found Jeremiah early the next morning. He wasn't in the gym, where he normally trained. He was down at Silver Pond, training on the bank next to the water. I stayed and watched him for a while. He was doing those exercises you always do on the jetty, using that sword you gave him. I wasn't going to say anything, just sneak away and pretend like I hadn't seen, because I figured he'd gone there for some privacy. Only then he looked up toward me, and I saw his face. I didn't think I'd ever seen anyone look so lonely.

"So I took him out to breakfast, and I asked how his date went. We talked, Jeremiah and me, a lot. About life in Deepwater, about everything that's happened. And Jeremiah said that the only person he ever felt could truly understand what he'd gone through was you. That the only time he truly felt like he could be himself was when he was talking to you. He said that when he'd gone out on the date with my friend, he'd realized halfway through that all he wanted to talk about was you, and how unfair that was to anyone else." She smiles at Callie. "I guess we both realized that this life we all lead—it isn't something you can just invite a stranger into. We're bound together, Callie. Jeremiah is bound to you, by all you've shared and seen together. He's never going to trust someone else like he does you. That's what he's realized this year, Callie. That when it comes down to it, there isn't anyone else for him. There never will be. You and Jeremiah are meant to be, Callie. I know it."

Avery doesn't wait for a reply, just touches Callie on the arm and walks away toward the kitchen. I'm thinking of how best to extricate myself when Callie emerges in front of me, her face flushed, eyes glittering. "I know you heard all that. I saw you standing there."

"I'm sorry. I thought about leaving, but I was worried Avery would say something to upset you. She didn't, though." I smile at her. "You must be happy, Callie."

"Happy?" Callie stares at me. "Why would that make me happy, Harper?"

"To know that Jeremiah loves you?" I'm confused. "I thought that was what you wanted."

"It is what I wanted. What I do want. But that isn't what Avery said." I realize with a shock that Callie isn't excited. She's angry. "Don't you see, Harper? Jeremiah doesn't want to be with me because he loves me. He wants to be with me by default—

because I'm the only girl he knows who actually understands the life he's come from. Jeremiah isn't in love with me. I'm just what he has to settle for, because he thinks every other option is cut off. And if you think I'm going to be with someone who sees me as a default option they've had to settle for—then you really don't know me at all."

She turns before I can say anything in response, and a moment later, I hear her van taking off down the drive.

CHAPTER 11

SEESAW

Callie doesn't come home that night, or the next morning. She sends a text to say she's staying with Cass and Connor. Two days pass during which Jeremiah doesn't leave the mansion, looking up every time a car comes up the road. I'm at war with myself as to whether or not to say anything to him, and just as torn over what I should or shouldn't tell Antoine. My dilemma is made no easier by Antoine being doubly kind and attentive, ensuring I want for nothing as the day of the equinox looms in front of us. When he leaves to hunt, he does it quickly and is nearly always back when I wake. He rarely leaves my side and is so gentle it breaks my heart and makes my ongoing deception even worse. A thousand times I think I should at least ask Iara, force her to confirm my suspicions. So long as it is in my head, though, I can pretend, at least to myself, that I'm technically not lying. The moment she confirms it aloud, I am deceiving Antoine, and although I know it is semantics, I cling to the distinction for the sake of my own sanity.

"I spoke to Callie," Avery tells me. It's only two days until the equinox, and the atmosphere in the mansion is growing more tense and expectant with every passing hour. "I told her Jeremiah only wants her. So where is she? And why does he still look like someone stabbed his favorite puppy?"

"I know you did. This isn't on you, Avery. It's something Callie has to work through herself."

"Well, she'd better hurry up. It isn't fair to string Jeremiah along like that. He's a good person." I can't help but laugh at the role reversal. "Only a few months ago, it was Callie standing in front of me, saying the exact same thing about you," I say.

"Yeah." Avery smiles ruefully. "I guess you're right."

Nonetheless, when Jeremiah knocks on my bedroom door not long afterward, I can't help but take Avery's point. His face is drawn and strained. "Have you seen Callie?" he asks without preamble.

"No, Jeremiah, I haven't. She sent a message to say she's at Cass's, though, if you want to go and see her."

"Do you know why she left?" His eyes narrow as he watches me. "If something happened, please tell me, Harper."

Suddenly, probably because of my own predicament, I'm impatient with games and lies. "Avery spoke to her," I tell him. "She told Callie what you'd said, that Callie is the only girl you truly trust and feel comfortable with."

Jeremiah frowns. "And Callie was upset by that?"

"Callie was upset because she thought that your shared secrets are the only reason you like her. Her pride was hurt, Jeremiah. I think her words were that she doesn't want to be your 'default option.' She wants to be your first choice."

"But she *is* my first choice!" Jeremiah looks completely taken aback. "I don't love Callie because of all this." He gestures around at the mansion. "I love her because she's the only girl I can ever imagine loving. I even went out on a date—more than one—and all I could talk about was her. All I could think about was that those girls weren't her."

"I know." I touch his arm. "I know, Jeremiah."

"Well, why doesn't she?"

"I think you'll just have to find a way of showing her."

"How do I do that?"

"I don't know." I watch him with sympathy as he strides to the door. "I guess that's the fun of it all. You have to work it out as you go." He shoots me a somewhat strained smile as he leaves, almost knocking into Antoine as he does.

"What's with him?" Antoine says as he comes in, closing the door behind him. I fill him in on the situation. "Ah." Antoine stretches out on the bed beside me, one arm behind his head. "Well. That will keep them both busy for a while. What?" he says laughingly, as I hit him. "We all have to make sacrifices for love, don't we?"

And that's it. One moment I'm laughing, and the next, the seesaw inside me has tipped, his words throwing the head side to the ground with a thud of finality I can't fight.

We all have to make sacrifices for love.

Guidry's voice in my head: . . .

"Antoine." I sit up and look at him. Dust motes dance in the afternoon sun filtering through the open window. The air is filled with the rich scents of spring and the lazy sound of whip-poor-wills trilling in the oak.

"I'm listening." He turns to rest his head on one arm, the golden flecks in his eyes warm among the cobalt.

"It was your blood that activated the Abatey inside me."

"I remember, Harper," he says, raising his eyebrows. "I was there at the time, if you'll recall."

"Well, I was wondering: if your blood activated Guidry and the pack, do you still feel them inside you?"

His brow creases faintly. "Do you mean do I feel them, like I do Tate?"

I nod. "Yes. Is it the same? Do you feel the same connection with those you activated as you do as a Maker? Do you feel it with me?"

He doesn't answer immediately, just watches me. Finally he says, "Why are you asking me this now, Harper?"

"I guess I just want to know." I meet his eyes. "Because for me, it feels as if you are still inside me. Not just because of the twins, or because I love you. I feel you, in my veins. In my being." It's easier, now that I'm putting it into words. "I guess I wonder if it will be different, after."

He reaches up, twining a lock of hair around his finger. "You're asking if the bond between Maker and vampire will feel different than what is already between us." He nods slowly. "Well, the answer is that I don't know if what is between us is the same as it is for Guidry and me, or the wolves, or even Tate. Your blood came into my body when I was almost drained to death, Harper. It literally brought every cell back to life, to the point where I was, for all intents and purposes, alive—human— for a time. It changed me forever, just as it did Cass. Even now I can still feel you inside me, feel a connection stronger than any I've known, even with Keziah. And as for my blood inside you, Harper—to be honest, my answer is that I don't know. I am so connected to you, my heart so entwined with yours, that I no longer know what the substance of that connection is. I do know it isn't just blood that binds us. I believe that even if all my senses were gone, still I would know how to find you, no matter where in the world you were. I may not be able to hear your voice in my head. But I can feel your essence in my heart. There is a certain presence you have that is yours and belongs to nobody else. I believe I would know that anywhere, whether you were vampire or human." He strokes my hair between thumb and forefinger, still looking at me from the pillow. "As to what that bond will be after I make you immortal, I won't pretend it doesn't frighten me, almost as much as the thought of that little shaman becoming part of your soul." His lips tighten and I see the effort he exerts to relax them. "I've seen so many bonds between Maker and vampire twist the relationship, turn it into something unhealthy. But I love you. And, I hope, at least, that you love me too." He gives me a half smile. "So I guess I have to believe that the bond we already have will simply deepen. I hope it does."

"You're afraid that it might not?" I stare at him curiously. "Why did you never say that before?"

He lifts the shoulder he isn't lying on. "What good would it do? We've agreed I will turn you. Even if you hate me once I do, at least the bond of hate will be with me—not someone else, like Tate. You should see your face," he laughs, touching my nose, and I'm glad the shadows are falling so he can't see the sudden bolt of terror behind my eyes and guess at its cause. He gathers me close and draws me down so my back is to him, his hands resting on my belly. "To answer your question," he says in my ear, "I'm aware of Guidry and the wolves. They're supernatural creatures, immortal because of my blood. With humans, my connection to them usually disappears after a few days. But Guidry and the others—yes, I feel them. Not in the same way as I do Tate. Nor do I have dominion over them, as Keziah did with me before I drank your blood and broke the connection. But I can feel them, yes. Like an instinct, a faint awareness in my body. I sense them. Where they are, how they feel. If I want to tune into that, I can."

"Can you do that with me?" I whisper, my hands covering his own. It suddenly feels so important that he can, something I can cling to, amid the lie I know I have to live. "Can you tune into me?"

"I've never been able to do that." Antoine's arms tighten around me. "You have always been a mystery to me, Harper. Perhaps it is the Abatey in you. We are connected, yes, as I told you before. But it isn't the same as with the others. I can sense you. But I can't be in your head, your heart, as I can with them. I can only sense you." His hands entwine with mine. "I hope that doesn't change," he murmurs against my hair. "I hope whatever binds us after this, strong as it is, doesn't change the bond we have. I don't know what I would do if I couldn't sense you within me, and myself within you."

I hold his arms close about me as dusk grows, watching the stars come out in the moon-dark night, and again, the truth rises in me like a tide, then recedes again, settling within me uneasily.

In two more days, it will be the equinox.

CHAPTER 12

NEWBORNS

The day before the equinox, I'm in the rear salon resting when a truck pulls in by the front porch. The pagoda was finished yesterday, and the house has been quiet today, everyone resting and gathering their strength for what we will face tomorrow. I'm surprised when I hear Connor and Remy's voices, then Guidry's lower, rougher tones. I'm still drifting in and out of sleep when I hear another vehicle and more voices. Tate and Iara are here too. The conversation is becoming heated. I struggle toward wakefulness and waddle into the kitchen, rubbing my eyes.

"What's going on?"

Everyone stops talking at once, and it's clear that there was something of an argument going on.

"Harper." Antoine rubs a hand over his face. "I thought you were upstairs."

"I was. I came downstairs, but I sat down in the salon and drifted off." I look around at the strained faces. "What's going on?" I ask again.

"It's Keziah," Remy says.

"Remy!" Frowning, Guidry shakes his head.

"It's better if Harper knows the truth." Antoine steps forward and takes my hands. "The wolves caught Keziah's scent last night. She has two newborns with her. The wolves chased them to the boundary of their land, but they are still close by. They went to ground when the sun came up."

"Only two?" I turn to Remy. "Are you sure about that?"

"Exactly!" Guidry throws his hand out and turns exasperated eyes to Antoine. "Like I said, it's naive in the extreme to think there are only two newborns. Did it not occur to anyone that she came onto our territory and showed us those two in order to deliberately mislead us as to her real strength?"

"And I'm saying that we should defend against what we know we are going to face," Connor interjects. "Keziah is on the pack's side of the river. The newborns can't enter the mansion, not without an invitation. But Keziah can. She was held here for centuries, and when the binding was broken, it didn't seem to affect her—so we have to assume she isn't kept out as normal vampires are. That makes her the most likely to try to take Harper and the twins. If she can't cross the river, she can't get to them. We need to hold her there."

"If she does manage to get a hold of the twins, Keziah will have us all in her power." Guidry glares at him. "That has to be her objective, which means she has a plan that I am willing to stake my last dollar involves more than just two newborns. Leaving only Takatoka and me to guard the land entrance is foolish. If there are more newborns, we won't know until they're on top of us." His eyes slide to Tate, who is watching the exchange quietly, and away again. Guidry's contemptuous expression makes abundantly clear that he does not enjoy their temporary alliance.

"We didn't catch the scent of any others." Connor folds his arms. "As far as we know, there are only three."

"And Keziah has proven herself cunning time and time

again." Guidry turns back to Antoine. "You've fought enough battles to know it's better to never underestimate an enemy."

"Guidry is right," says Cass quietly, shooting Connor an apologetic glance. "You know how Keziah thinks, Antoine. She didn't let the pack find her by accident. She wants us to know she is here. Which means it's likely there are also things she doesn't want us to know."

Antoine's face is tight. "We don't have unlimited resources, Cass. You and I are the only ones I know for sure Keziah can't exert control over. Iara is the only one with midwife experience. Tate and Guidry know the land around the mansion better than anyone else and are two of our most experienced fighters. Unless something has changed, newborns can't enter the mansion without an invitation, which means that so long as the twins are inside it, they are safe." He pauses, then continues, a finger unfolding for each point, as if reciting a mental list. "The wolves are best placed on their own land, where they are at their strongest. I don't want to risk more resources at the mansion on a maybe, when we know for certain that Keziah and two newborns are coming over the river. Harper will be at her most vulnerable while she is being turned.

"Keziah was watching our land when the wolves caught her scent. That means she's seen the platform that has been built there. She knows enough of pagan worship to know what it is, even if she didn't see the Warao shaman sleeping on it." He looks around the room as he finishes his summary. "That is where it is most likely she will come for Harper."

A short silence greets this conclusion, and I see that everyone is working through his words in their own minds. It's Guidry who breaks it, his tone flat and hard. "Then you're going to leave the land approach unguarded but for Takatoka and me. Aren't you forgetting something?" Guidry folds his arms and glares around the room. "I'm going to say it, since it seems nobody else will."

I tense, knowing what is coming. By the dark look on Antoine's face, he does, too.

Guidry clicks his tongue impatiently. "The newborns will only be held at bay so long as Harper is alive." A tense silence fills the kitchen. Nobody looks at me. "Well?" Guidry demands, looking around. "Tell me I'm wrong."

Nobody does.

"So what happens after that?" Guidry looks around at us. "How do we stop a pack of newborns from coming through the door if Harper is dead?"

Jeremiah steps forward. "We'll have frankincense burning everywhere. And I'll be there," he says quietly.

"Me, too," says Iara. "And Callie—she will be with the twins in the room. I may not be able to fight as well as you, Guidry, but I'm still a vampire. I can protect the twins if it comes to it." Guidry's eyes rest on her briefly, not with any warmth. He seems to regard Iara with the same contempt he does Tate, though he hides it slightly better.

"Frankincense is a last line of defense," he says curtly. His eyes cut to Antoine. "And we've both seen it overcome before."

Antoine has his head bent, so I can't see his face, but I can feel his tension. Guidry glances around the room and frowns.

"Where is Callie?" he says, directing the question to Jeremiah. "She should be here, too."

Again, I find myself touched by Guidry's consideration. Both Jeremiah and Callie are so often relegated to the background in discussions such as these. Guidry, though, seems always to take the time to include them. Now Jeremiah nods, giving Guidry a grateful look. "I'll call her," he says, and I suspect he is grateful for the excuse to do so. He pulls out his phone and I hear him say Callie's name as he steps out onto the porch.

"Can someone explain to me how frankincense can be overcome?" I look around the room. Tate visibly blanches but doesn't reply. Both he and Guidry look at Antoine, as if waiting for his permission to explain.

"I'm not saying you're wrong, Guidry." Antoine is leaning against the sink, arms folded over his chest and legs crossed at the ankle, frowning at the wall opposite. His eyes cut to me then move away. "Frankincense can be overcome by compulsion," he says flatly. "It's horrific, the kind of torture no creature should ever endure—but it can be done. It's one of the reasons for making newborns. They can be compelled by their Maker to endure any amount of pain in order to achieve an objective." His face hardens. "Of course, there are very few, even of our kind, with the stomach for such sadism."

"But Keziah is one of them," I say quietly.

Antoine tilts his head in passive agreement. After a moment, he looks back at Guidry. "The only alternative is to put the mansion in Connor's name. Or Jeremiah's."

"That won't work." I shake my head decisively, and they all look at me. "Well, it won't," I say defensively. "Jeremiah is human. Frankincense or not, we don't know that Keziah can't compel him. And Connor is a supernatural creature." I look around. "Somehow I think you all know that means that his name on the deed won't keep vampires out." None of them answer me. Guidry tilts his head and glares into the distance, but he doesn't argue, which I take it means he knows I'm right. "I thought so." I look around the room. "But I can't be compelled, by anyone. And, yes"—I turn to Guidry—"you're right. I can't protect the twins after I'm dead. But all we must do is hold the newborns at bay for long enough for me to rise and face Keziah." I look around the kitchen, seeing the discomfort and doubt on their faces, the stony mask on Antoine's. "I can beat her, Antoine," I say quietly. "I know I can."

The reality is that I know no such thing, but something deep inside me rebels against signing the mansion over to anyone else. "This is my home." My voice is both louder and more forceful than I had expected. "It's our home." I gesture to Connor. "Ours. Callie's. Jeremiah's. Antoine's." I touch my belly. "It's their home, too." Unexpected tears blur my eyes. "I can't sign it away. It's just—wrong." My voice breaks off, unable to express what I mean.

There's a moment of uncomfortable silence, then Antoine carries on as if I haven't spoken at all. "The other option is to leave Connor with you and Tate, Guidry."

His matter-of-fact tone effectively closes the matter to debate, and I think gratefully that in this moment I might love him more than I ever have, particularly when I see him meet Guidry's mutinous expression with the hard flint that we all know is immutable. Guidry subsides, and Antoine turns to my brother, raising his eyebrows. "It would give Guidry and Tate an advantage to have a wolf at their side. Particularly one that can't be killed by Keziah."

"No," Connor says flatly. "I'll be on this side of the river, near Cass and near the platform where Harper will be turned. If more newborns come from the land approach, I won't be far. But I will fight beside Cass."

Guidry takes in his set expression and Antoine's frown and sighs. "Well, it is what it is." He casts Tate a dark look. "It seems it's just you and me, Serpent."

Tate inclines his head politely but doesn't answer. Jeremiah puts his head around the door. "Callie was already on her way here. That's her coming in the driveway now." Guidry glares around the room. "Think I'll go explain the plan to her," he says coldly. "Seems to me she has more sense than most of you." He stomps out to the porch. Connor and Cass fall into conversation with Remy and move out to the back porch. Katiusca calls to Iara from the back door. Casting Tate a rather exasperated look, she goes to see what the shaman wants.

Antoine raises his eyebrows at Tate, who smiles ruefully. "Iara is finding Katiusca's demands a little wearing," he says. "I think we'll all be glad when this is over." He looks apologetically at me. "No offense, Harper."

"None taken." I smile at him. "I hope you know how grateful I am, Tate, to you and Iara, for all you've done to help us. I know it can't be easy, especially given the tension between you and Guidry."

Tate's smile fades. "On that matter," he says, looking out the window where Guidry and Callie are just visible, walking around the side of the mansion, out of immediate earshot. "Are you entirely sure you can trust Guidry, Antoine?"

I stiffen. Antoine's mouth tightens. "Not you, too." He glares at Tate. "It's difficult enough to manage Guidry's hostility without you adding to it. The man has good reason to hate you, Tate, but that's no reason to doubt his loyalty."

"Don't you think it's strange, though?" Tate persists. "He has no real reason to care so much about protecting us. But here he is, and if you haven't noticed, he seems more interested in protecting the twins than in anything else. I'm just saying that perhaps you might want to think about what other motivations he might have."

Antoine's eyes have narrowed to thin strips of flint during this speech, and he's grown increasingly still. When he answers Tate, it's in a voice I haven't heard him use since the early days of Tate's return to Deepwater.

"Guidry and I have fought together more times than you've even thought of raising steel. He has saved my life—not once, but many times. On one of those occasions, both of our lives came at the cost of someone else's: the first woman Guidry loved since you took his wife and children from him." Tate pales as Antoine continues in the same unrelenting tone. "To my knowledge, in the two hundred years since then, Guidry has never so much as looked at another woman. And yet his friendship with me, and his loyalty, have never once wavered. He is here because of that friendship, and for no other reason." He steps closer, his eyes boring into Tate's. "So when you ask me if I trust him, I will say this: you and I, Tate, are bound by ties of family and blood. By a Maker's bond and, yes, even if belatedly, by friendship. But Guidry and I?" He tilts his head sharply, lips pressing into a hard line. "Guidry and I are brothers of the heart," he says softly. "Brothers born of war and sacrifice. I would trust Guidry de Ainhoa with my last breath. And you—*brother*—you would do well to never question Guidry's allegiance again. Are we clear?"

Tate's face is ashen, his eyes desolate and pained as a bleak winter sky. "We're clear," he says quietly. He does not speak again but leaves the room, his figure stiff, sad, and aged in a way I could not have imagined.

Antoine stares after him, then exhales in a rush and rubs his face with his hand, cursing under his breath. Finally he looks at me, his eyes hooded. "Go ahead," he says roughly. "I know. First Guidry, now Tate. For the second time this week, I shouldn't have done that."

"And I know you'll make it right." He looks at me in surprise. "So does Tate, even if he's hurt. He knows you're not yourself right now." I shrug. "None of us are. And he knows *you*, Antoine, just like Guidry does. He will forgive you." Antoine makes a hard noise and looks away, his mouth tight with what I know is self-recrimination.

I touch his arm. "Thank you," I say softly. "For doing that, back there. About the mansion being in my name." My throat closes over again, cutting off my words.

He covers my hand with his own. His mouth twists into a familiar, wry smile. "It wasn't entirely sentimental." He meets my eyes and lifts a shoulder in a half apology. "Your magic is tied to this ground. I'm not taking any chances with that. Better we fight off a whole army of newborns than mess with whatever devilry that damned shaman is planning." But there is a softness behind his eyes, and whatever he says, I know he feels it too.

The mansion is our home. And I won't let anyone, not even Keziah and her mad progeny, take it from us.

We've fought too hard for it. All of us. The mansion isn't just a building. It's our past and our future, the place where the bones of those we love feed the earth.

It's home. And no matter how insane our lives may be, or perhaps because of it, that means something to me.

It means *everything* to me.

I think of Guidry, suddenly, of his words to me, and of what he himself has learned to live with, all because he loved someone so much that even despite losing her, he has always respected her choice. Somehow, I know that whoever that woman was, she never gave Guidry the option to talk her out of what she knew she must do. And though I will never meet her and don't even know her name, I can see the power of her sacrifice in the man he has become. I sense it has defined him in powerful ways, perhaps even brought him to the point where he is here, fighting for Antoine and Antoine's children, still bound by that love.

It might be a lie, holding the truth to myself. But that is my choice—and my own sacrifice, for both Antoine and our children. I know that the only way I can defeat Keziah is with Iara as my Maker. But asking Antoine to accept that is a step too far. He might never forgive me for the lie—but better I give us all a chance to survive this than allow him to change my mind, even if it means I lose him forever.

I stand up and walk into his arms, and for the first time since I realized the truth of how I will be transformed, I know what to do and feel at peace.

Then I remember Tate's face.

"Make sure you fix it with Tate," I murmur, my voice muffled by his chest.

I feel him smile against my head. "I will."

We stay like that for a long time, standing at the window and looking out together—at my magical garden, at the river beyond, and at the strange, wooden pagoda, where soon enough, my life will end and another will begin.

Night is coming, and tomorrow will be the equinox.

CHAPTER 13

DEPTHS

In the early hours of the morning, I look out the window, at the platform by my garden.

Antoine has gone hunting, and the mansion is quiet. The night is moon dark, the pagoda and platform below barely visible as more than a shadow. Despite the gloom, I can make out a lithe figure moving in a slow, rhythmic dance across the boards. It is Katiusca. I wonder if he's already beginning the dance that will bring in the magic of the four-headed serpent tonight, when my transformation takes place. As I watch, the figure flits to each corner of the platform, raising something. He isn't dancing, I realize. He's putting in place the kanobotuma, the representations of the Warao deities that must sit at each corner.

For a moment, I feel drawn to him and wonder if I should go down and try to talk to him. Soon enough, he will be part of my own soul. Somehow it seems as if we should have more than a passing acquaintance. But I'm tired, and the hour is late, and he feels strange and far away. When I think of him becoming a part of me, I feel lonely and afraid. My arms cradle the babies sleeping inside me. Selfishly, for now I just want to be human. I want to treasure every last moment I'm still *me*, the Harper who was once Tessa's twin and who fell in love with Antoine. Something tells me that soon enough, the Harper I am now will be nothing more than a distant memory. And if I dwell on that thought for long, it terrifies me.

I stand at the window until first light is a clear thread across the sky. Katiusca turns to watch it, facing me across the length of the lawn. It is his final dawn, I realize with a shock. The last time he will be alive to see the sun rise. The last time either of us will.

Despite the distance, I sense he knows I am there, that we are sharing this final sunrise together. We stand in silence, together yet apart, as the day grows into being. When the sun has risen above the trees and glimmers on the river, Katiusca raises one hand in a silent salute. I return it, and we stand there, facing each other across the still dawn, sharing the last one we will see as two individual beings. Finally, he nods once and turns away. Lying down on the floorboards, he pulls the blankets over his head.

I give the dawn a last look, and then I too go back to bed. I fall into a deep, dreamless sleep—the last one of my human life.

I WAKE TO THE MIDDAY SUN AND VOICES ON THE SLOPE BELOW MY window.

"I've been watching you train in the mornings." It's Guidry's voice. "You know how to fight."

"I've been training since I was a kid," Callie answers. "I'm not great, but I can hold my own."

"It may come to that tonight. If it does, once Iara takes Harper down to the platform, you will be the only one in that room with the twins." Callie is silent. "You've already been thinking of that, haven't you," Guidry says, and there's a grudging respect in his voice. "Good. Then it's time for me to give you this."

Curious, I pull myself out of bed and go to the window. Guidry has a knife in his hand, the steel edge flashing in the sunlight. I recognize its carved handle: it's the knife he showed Callie and me, when he told us the story of the night he met Madame Lysette. "It might be old," he says now, turning it in his hand, "but Duval, the man who made it, had, shall we say, special talents. He wrought frankincense into the metal itself as it was forged. Don't ask me how; it was a secret the man took to his grave, unfortunately. But among those who knew of such things, his blades were famous. They are rare indeed now. He made this one especially for me, and it has served me well." He turns the blade in the sunlight. "However, given that tonight I will be in wolf form, it seems it will be of more value in your hand." He hands Callie the knife. "Something tells me you will use it wisely."

Callie takes the knife and stares at it, turning it over in her hand. When she looks up at Guidry, though, her face is hard rather than flattered.

"Why are you giving this to me? Why is it you're so damn sure I'm the right person to stay with Harper?" She looks away. "What if I can't protect her?" Her voice has dropped slightly, more lost than angry, as it was a moment ago, her old accent rising again. "I got no powers. Comes to it, I can't put up any real fight against wolves, or vampires. Not for long, at least." She shakes her head. "You're out here, talkin' at me like I'm some kinda equal, when you and I both know that when it comes down to it, chances are I ain't seein' any daylight tomorrow."

And there it is, I think, my heart twisting unbearably. I can't stand the thought that she is so scared, prepared to risk so much. I'm about to put my head out the window to interrupt them, put a stop to her being involved at all, when Guidry grips her arms and speaks with an odd intensity that makes me pause. "Do you trust me, Callie?"

Callie stiffens. "I don' trust nobody."

"Which is exactly why you're the right person to do this." He shakes her slightly. "I've lived a long time, Callie. I've learned to recognize qualities other people might not see. In this instance, I think everyone here underestimates both you and Jeremiah. I can see that you will do what you must—will tackle everything that lies before you." He steps back, releasing her arms, his tone lightening. "I believe you both have talents, Callie. Believe me when I say you will do extraordinary things together. Things that will change lives. Save them, too."

"You seem real sure of that." Callie sounds skeptical.

Guidry gives her a twisted grin. "Let's just say that living so long makes a man impatient with human self-doubt. Your time on this earth is too short to doubt yourself, Callie. Believe in your own skills, and live the life you dare." He laughs softly. "And if you ever tell anyone I gave you such hippieish advice, I will never forgive you. Now"—he nods briskly, changing the tone of the conversation—"tell me what you and Jeremiah have already planned." Callie gives him a hard, assessing look then, taking a deep breath, nods.

"I gave Jeremiah a sword like mine before he went away to college," she begins. "He's not bad with it now, though not as good as me. Tonight, both our swords will be covered in frank-incense oil. One deep cut will be enough to at least incapacitate a vampire for a while. I've made grenades of frankincense water, too. I've been drinking frankincense-infused water for months, and I'm sure Jeremiah has too." She pauses. "We won't be caught unprepared, if that's what you're concerned about."

"I'm less worried than I was five minutes ago." Guidry gives a cough of laughter. "And the knife I gave you—make sure you carry it on you at all times. I truly believe it may be your best chance of survival tonight. Will you do that?"

Callie nods, tucking the knife away safely.

"And there's something else I wanted to talk to you about."

"Oh?"

"The pendants Harper wears around her neck," he says, his voice low. "Do you understand what they are?" My hand flies to the three small pendants on chains around my neck. Two are small bottles encased in silver filigree, talismans that Tessa told me I must always wear so long as I am pregnant, and that I must give to the twins as soon as they are born. They hold blood, I know, though whose I'm not entirely sure. The third pendant is the vial I once made beneath a full moon, containing mine and Antoine's blood. It helped me travel back in time after I visited Tessa, and I have kept it close; it feels powerful to me, reassuring, somehow.

Tessa told me the two small pendants serve as anchors to the twins, a way for them to find their way back to Antoine and me. It's a measure of how deep Antoine's trust in Guidry is, I think, listening to Guidry now, that he has told him of their purpose.

"I know what they are," Callie is saying.

"Then you know they must be given to the twins the moment they are born."

"I do." Callie's voice is wary.

"I've been around long enough to know more than I care to about newborn vampires." Guidry's voice is hard. "I don't want to sound alarmist, but might I suggest you make absolutely certain the twins are wearing those pendants before Iara takes Harper out of the room? None of us knows what Harper might become after that little shaman does his magic. I'd rather be certain Antoine's daughters are safe before that happens."

"You have my word." The wariness is gone from Callie's voice. "And don't worry. Harper has already told Iara the same thing. We'll make sure the pendants are left with the twins when Iara takes Harper. None of us wants to risk anything happening to those girls."

I'm touched once again at the depths hiding within Guidry. I can see why he and Antoine have been friends so long. I am unbearably grateful that, despite knowing the dangers of what I will become, still he has respected my right to make my own choices—while also doing all he can to protect our twins, and Antoine himself. The fact that he puts their safety above all other concerns touches me to the core. That he, too, sees what I do in both Callie and Jeremiah makes me even more grateful for his presence. If anyone deserves to have people to believe in her, it's Callie.

Guidry puts a hand on Callie's shoulder. "Have faith," he says quietly. "I don't doubt you will do all that is asked of you tonight —and more besides."

"Thank you," breathes Callie, and even from my window I can see the glow in her cheeks, the look of shy gratitude she gives Guidry. With a shock, I realize that even though he has been alive for centuries, on the surface Guidry is no older than Antoine. He's also devastatingly handsome, with his shock of black hair and lean, almost-emaciated face, the livid scar at his throat only adding to his rakish appeal. *I wonder*, I think, looking between Guidry and Callie. Could it be that after all these years, Guidry has finally found someone else to love?

A moment later, I realize I might not be the only one to whom that thought has occurred.

"Callie?" I hear Jeremiah's voice on the porch beneath me, and a moment later he steps onto the lawn, coming to stand by Callie's side. "I think Antoine is looking for you, Guidry," he says, regarding the older man with a distinctly frosty expression. "He's down by the river."

Guidry, seeming not remotely concerned by Jeremiah's manner, grins at them both and lopes off down the lawn. I revise my earlier suspicions. Guidry doesn't seem in the least upset by Jeremiah's arrival, and in fact, I'd swear he gave Jeremiah a conspiratorial wink as he left. Which means he offered his knife to Callie because he really does trust her and admires her fighting skills. Somehow, that makes me like him even more.

"There wasn't no need to be rude." Callie glares at Jeremiah, her exaggerated Memphis accent a sure signal she is upset.

"Wasn't there?" Jeremiah's voice has an unaccustomed edge to it. "Do you have a special liking for that wolf, Callie?"

"And what if I do?" Callie takes a step away from him, her slender body uncharacteristically stiff. "It didn't bother you none when I used to train with Guidry, before you went away to college."

"Well, that was before I realized—" He stops abruptly.

"Before you realized what, Jeremiah?" Callie stares at him. "That I'm the only human girl livin' in the same world of vampires and wolves as you?"

"Not only that," says Jeremiah, clearly taken aback.

"Not only that? Oh, wait—and also that you quite like my company, right? That thought came a long-distant second, I'm guessing."

"Wait a minute, Callie." Jeremiah catches her arm, but Callie twists out of his grip with an easy move. "Wait," Jeremiah says again. "Tell me the truth. Is there something between you and Guidry?"

"Why do you care?" Callie flings the words at him, hurt catching her voice. "You and I are friends, Jeremiah—and we ain't nothing more than that. Just 'cause we're the only two humans in a supernatural world don't make us somehow destined for each other. Neither of us should mistake this for something it ain't. You should have your first choice, whoever that may be. And you're young still; maybe you ain't even met her yet." Callie wipes an angry arm over her face and takes a deep breath. When she speaks again, her voice has a quiet dignity. "And I deserve to *be* someone's first choice, Jeremiah.

Not the second option you settle for, just 'cause this life means you can't have nothin' else."

Jeremiah stares at her, his face pale. "Then you do like him," he says, his voice low and angry. "All this time, it's been Guidry?"

Callie stares at him for a long moment. "You know something, Jeremiah?"

He doesn't answer, just shrugs angrily.

"You're an idiot."

Turning toward the mansion, she stomps up the stairs, leaving Jeremiah on the lawn staring after her.

I move back from the window before he can notice me. Eavesdropping, I think guiltily, is becoming a habit. Hearing Callie's footsteps on the stairs, I hastily go to shower before she realizes I was listening in. When I come out, she's sitting on the window seat, staring moodily down the slope at where Jeremiah is standing with Antoine and Guidry. Even from here I can see hostility in every line of his body as he looks at the wolf. The sun has gone behind a layer of purple cloud that rises over the river like a stage curtain.

"Jeremiah thinks that I like Guidry." She says it abruptly, not looking at me. I'm searching for an appropriate answer when she shoots me a sideways glance. "I know you were listening, Harper. I saw you at the window."

"I'm so sorry." I sit on the bed. "I didn't mean to. I heard Guidry talking about the pendants, and . . ."

"I don't care none about that." She waves me away. Her accent is still heavy enough to tell me she is deeply hurt. "I don't mind that you were listening. I just want to know what you think."

"What I think about what?" I ask cautiously.

"You know 'bout what." She gives me an impatient look. "About Jeremiah. What he said. What I said."

"Do you like Guidry?"

"Of course not! Not like he thinks, anyway." Her face screws up. "And anyway—Guidry is *old*." Realizing what she's said, she reddens. "I mean, I know he's the same as Antoine, but it's different, you know? I mean, you and Antoine—you don't seem different in age at all . . . Oh, I don't know. I can't explain it."

"It's okay," I say, laughing. "I know what you mean. Guidry does seem older. Or unavailable, at least. Perhaps it's grief. He's suffered a great deal, and I get the feeling he never really got over a girl he loved a long time ago."

"Whatever," says Callie impatiently. I turn away to hide my smile. "Now Jeremiah thinks there's something going on between Guidry and me. And there's not."

"Well, maybe you should tell him there isn't," I say. "Games are never good, Callie. And you've told me before that Jeremiah is a good person who deserves to know the truth. Maybe you should just tell him how you feel."

"But what if the truth isn't the right thing?" She looks at me, her eyes dark with hurt. "If Jeremiah really does feel that way 'bout me, then why was he so easily put off by the thought that there might be something going on with Guidry? Maybe, deep down, he was relieved. And maybe his thinking that there's someone else is the best thing for both of us. This way he can go back to college and forget about all of this, meet someone new."

"And what about you?" I ask gently. "What will you do when Jeremiah meets someone else?"

"I'll be busy enough here as it is. We'll have twins to look after." She gives me a watery smile and stands up. I put my arms out to give her a hug and feel a strange rush of warmth. Callie looks down at the floorboards and her mouth makes a perfect *O*. Her eyes come back up to mine.

"Harper," she says slowly, "I think your water just broke."

CHAPTER 14

EQUINOX

I'm pacing across the wooden floorboards when Antoine bursts into the room.

"Is she alright? What's happening?" His face is white with worry. "Harper. I'm here. Are you okay? How do you feel?"

"Fine." I laugh shakily. "Really, Antoine. I'm fine. Nothing is happening yet, not really. I'm just restless. Iara says walking will help." I put my hand on his arm. "You don't need to stay. Do what you need to." I'm lying. Right now, I want nothing more than to hold on to Antoine and never let go. I'm terrified. If I think for a moment about the hours that lie ahead, I fear I will break down entirely. But so long as I focus on what is happening in my body, on walking from one side of my bedroom to the other, I'm okay.

"Shouldn't you be in the other room?" Antoine asks worriedly.

"Not yet. I'll go when it's closer." *Or not at all*, I think but don't say. Every time I look at the other room, with its bank of machines and clinical equipment, I feel sick and afraid. For now, I'm fine just where I am. Iara seems no less keen than I am to go into the other room.

"Plenty of babies born without all of that," she'd said dismissively when she saw it.

"The obstetrician is less than a mile from here," Antoine says. He's definitely a fan of modern medicine. "And she's not going anywhere. I have her compelled to be awake with her phone charged."

"What on earth is she doing?" I ask, curious.

He gives me a tight smile. "Enjoying an all-expenses-paid stay on a luxury houseboat, that for some mysterious reason, is absolutely not moving anywhere tonight other than the old Harrison jetty it's tied to. She can be here in ten minutes, less if necessary. Just say the word," he says to Iara, who makes an impatient sound and rolls her eyes. "It will be many hours yet," she says.

"I have to go." Antoine holds my hands, his eyes roaming over my face. "I need to make sure everything is safe." He glances out the window, where the sun is starting to fall toward the river. The ominous layer of cloud has become a wall behind which the sun is just edging. The clouds are a strange shape, circular at the center like a spiral, while the outer edge glistens hard silver. "There's a storm coming," Antoine mutters, staring at it. "A bad one." He meets my eyes and I know we're thinking the same thing: that the storm has nothing to do with a Mississippi spring, and everything to do with an Abatey giving birth.

"I'll be fine," I say quietly, holding his eyes.

His hands come up to cup my face. "I'll see you at the platform, if not before," he says roughly. "And Harper, if you need me—if anything goes wrong—"

"I know." I cover his mouth with my hand, my eyes on his. "I know, Antoine."

Slowly he takes my hand away from his mouth, and then he kisses me, long, sweet, and yet all too brief. "I love you," he whispers. "Always, Harper. Don't forget that."

"And I love you." I touch the ring on his wedding finger. "Always, Antoine. Always and forever."

A sudden gust of wind blows an entire red magnolia flower into the room. The sun disappears behind the cloud bank, and in the sudden gloom, lit only by the gleam of my fairy lights, the red magnolia glistens like blood on the floor. I shiver and turn away from it. "Go," I say, touching his face.

He nods slowly, his eyes taking in the storm and the flower on the floor. Turning, he leaves the room, pausing briefly at the door. But instead of looking back, he takes a deep breath and stiffens his shoulders; then he is gone. A moment later, I hear him calling Guidry's name in a hard, authoritative voice.

I know that voice. My husband has gone to war.

"Now it is us." Iara comes to my side, putting her arm around my shoulders. "Women, as it should be. No place for men when babies are being born."

I smile at her. "Maybe where you come from. Here they deliver as many babies as women do."

"Ha!" Iara snorts disparagingly. "What do men know about babies? Do they carry them? Of course not. Ridiculous." She carries on in this vein for some time, a constant patter that I eventually realize is designed to distract me rather than be an actual conversation. I walk across the room and back, across and back, unable to stop, even though my body feels heavy and my feet are killing me. Outside, the wind has picked up. It feels hot and uneasy on my skin. The river is deep brown and restless. Flowers scatter across the grass, magnolias and moonflowers spreading white and red petals among the green. I can see Antoine and Cass standing by the water, feet spread wide, staring across the river to the bank on the other side, where I know the wolves are. The low, lean figure of Connor in wolf form prowls the riverbank between them, coming repeatedly to stand beside Cass.

Callie comes in. Her long sword is in a sheath strapped to

her back, and Guidry's knife is in a leather holder on her belt. "Jeremiah is in the kitchen," she says. "Guidry and Tate are outside. We're ready, Harper."

"I know you are." I reach out my hand and she takes it. I press her fingers gently. "I'm glad you're here, Callie."

"Of course." Callie tries to smile, but all I can see in her eyes is worry. "I will keep your twins safe, Harper. I promise I will."

"I know." I nod. "I know you will."

The first pain hits as the sun disappears. I straighten up and look out the window. In a small break in the clouds, I see the slim crescent of the new moon hovering just above the water. It glimmers briefly in the purple dusk, then slips behind the horizon.

Flames burst into life in the torches placed around the pagoda. Their flickering light illuminates Katiusca's dancing figure, whirling and leaping as if he were fire himself. Odd snatches of his chant are carried through my open window on gusts of wind. Iara goes to close the glass shutters.

"Don't," I say sharply. "Leave them open." I can't bear the thought of being closed off from Antoine, and from the night itself. I need to feel the air on my face, smell the raw river mud. "Tessa," I whisper, as I come close to the window. "Are you here?" The wind blows with such force it whips the hair around my face, and tears sting my eyes. "Stay with me," I murmur. "Don't leave me alone."

"I am here," says Iara, concern in her eyes, and I realize she thinks I am talking to her. I smile and nod, but Iara seems oddly distant. I feel as if everything is swirling away from me, or rather as if I'm spiralling further into myself with every contraction.

Iara and Callie try to make me lie down, but I don't want to. I keep walking, one side of the room to the other, pausing when the pains hit, gripping the wooden posts of my four-poster bed with such force it leaves dents in my skin. As I walk, I look out the window. Down on the platform, a strange mist is taking shape, odd swirls that glisten like smoke in the flaming torchlight.

"The serpent is coming," Iara whispers, following my eyes. Her face is fearful as she looks down at the platform and Katiusca's dancing figure. I stare at the mist, and when the next pain hits, I see the mist leap and surge, growing in size and density.

The night wears on, the pains coming gradually closer and with more intensity. I'm aware of Callie and Iara talking in low voices, wanting me to move into the other room, but I can't. I am exactly where I'm supposed to be. My world has shrunk to two points of focus: my body and the serpent growing on the platform below.

A contraction hits and I buckle at the knees, falling to the floor. Just as I hit the boards, I hear a savage snarling, then a warning howl on the night wind that I instinctively know is Guidry's.

"They're coming," I gasp.

Iara looks up at me with a reassuring smile. "*Si*, Harper," she says calmly. "Your babies are coming now."

But I'm not talking about my babies. I know the twins are coming, can feel them like a river tide that can't be held back. But I feel something else as well, a sharp, hungry danger on the night. "Keziah," I gasp, seeking out Callie with my eyes. "And the newborns. They're close."

"Let the others fight Keziah." Callie takes both of my hands in her own. "There's only you, Harper. You and your babies."

I can hear fighting in the distance, sharp cries and a wolf's low lethal growl, followed by a dull, sickening thud. Callie's eyes flicker over my head to the door behind me, and over the wind and pain I hear footsteps on the stairs. "Callie." It's Jeremiah's voice. "There are more newborns out there. Guidry got one, but another pulled him down, and there are more in the woods. Tate is still fighting, but we were right—they've been compelled. Frankincense won't hold them. You need to be ready."

"Callie!" This time the pain rips through me with a mind-bending intensity, and I scream aloud, my hands gripping Callie's so tightly I hear her gasp, though she doesn't pull away. "Go," I pant. "Help them."

"No." Callie is looking over my head at Jeremiah. "I can't leave her. Close the door, Jeremiah. Guard it."

"No!" I struggle, but the pain comes again, tearing me apart.

"Yes," says Iara, from somewhere else. "Now it is time. Push, Harper."

I don't need her to tell me to push; the need to do so is all-consuming. I close my eyes and see the mist from the platform, a gleaming, sinuous shape in the darkness of my mind, calling me forward. I open my eyes and see Callie's face, set and determined, above me. "Come on, Harper," she urges. "Push."

Beyond the door comes a fierce shriek, both savage and agonized.

The newborn vampires. I can't imagine the torture of being compelled to fight through a haze of frankincense; I have seen even a single inhalation cause Tate and Antoine severe pain.

There are the dull thuds and erratic thumps of combat, then a grunt of pain from Jeremiah. Callie's hands grip mine just as hard as I have hers, her face white. There is a crash against the door, and then another hoarse cry that sounds like Jeremiah, followed by the sound of splintering wood as something crashes through the wooden banister.

"Jeremiah!" calls Callie, her face terrified.

"Callie! I'm here!" Jeremiah roars in reply, and Callie closes her eyes in relief.

I take a deep breath.

"Tessa!"

I cry out my sister's name as I bear down. Wind rattles the roof, throwing open another pair of shutters that bang loudly against the wall. I can feel the serpent calling me from below, winding hungrily toward me. From somewhere far distant comes an unearthly yowl that sears my soul. It is Keziah, shrieking her fury at the death of one of her newborns.

"That's it!" Iara calls. "Another, Harper!" I push again, and I feel the small body slip from me, but I can barely open my eyes. I'm somewhere else, almost half gone, and I hardly notice when Callie pulls one of the pendants over my head. Somewhere close by, the sharp cry of an infant cuts the night, and my heart twists. One of my babies is here. *Aurelia.* I want to say her name, but I have no strength. A tear slides down my face. I want her, want my baby close to me; I feel bereft.

"Keep going," Iara orders, her voice sharp. "Keep going, Harper. You're nearly there."

I take another breath, and it seems the serpent is just outside my window now, calling me, trying to draw me forward. "Tessa," I say again, but this time the word is inaudible, and the answering wind at the window so weak it barely lifts the curtain.

"What's wrong with her?" I hear Callie's voice, low and urgent. "What's happening?"

"Callie!" Jeremiah shouts from outside the door. "There are more of them! You have to get Harper out of here!"

"Push, Harper!" Iara's voice is rising, and I can hear the fear in it. "Come on now!"

"What's *wrong* with her?" Fear sharpens Callie's words.

"She's fine. Come *on*, Harper!" Iara's voice is becoming shrill and urgent.

"She isn't fine!" Callie's voice comes from a distance. "Iara! Do something!"

I think hazily that there is something wrong with the lights, because they're fading into the darkness outside the window. In the black that settles around me, all I can see is the serpent's glistening shape, and then from somewhere close, I hear Tessa speak.

Harper. Tessa's voice is low and clear, inside me, around me. *Harper, you have to wake up. You have to push one more time, Harper, or your baby will die. Marguerite will die. Harper!*

"Harper! Can you hear me?" A gust of wind hits my face, and my eyes fly open to find Callie's terrified eyes staring down at me, and Iara yelling something I can't hear.

There is a savage cry, and behind me the door crashes open. Callie lets go of my hands and leaps to her feet in a crouch beside me, Guidry's knife in her hand, her other arm curled protectively around the tiny swaddled form in her arms. "Callie!" Jeremiah calls hoarsely. "Guidry—"

Callie throws Guidry's knife, and there is a sickening thud as it hits something made of flesh. There is a brief shriek and Callie steps forward, pulling the knife from the fallen figure. On the wild night comes another long, keening sound, as Keziah screams her fury once more.

My head goes back and my body seizes until, with a final, deadly push, I feel another weight leave my body, and I realize Keziah's scream has become my own, and my baby is born.

Marguerite.

Callie reappears beside me, the blade, now dripping with blood, back in her hand, her face ashen. The wolf I know as Guidry paces through the door and slips into human form as he falls to the floor beside me, his body covered in bites and cuts.

"The pendants, Callie!" he rasps. "Quickly!"

I stare up at Callie as she pulls the second pendant from my throat, but a film is falling over my eyes. I barely make out what is happening as Iara hands Callie Marguerite's tiny body.

"Get Harper out of here," Guidry roars at Iara, and I feel strong arms coming beneath me. "Hurry!"

As Iara leaps through the window, carrying me in her arms, she twists, and I have a clear view into the room.

Callie, pale-faced in the corner, is holding my two babies against her chest. Guidry, back in wolf form, is crouched in front of her, growling, while Tate and Jeremiah grim-faced, stand either side of him, facing the door. Callie holds the blood-soaked knife out before the babies in her arms. Jeremiah holds both her sword and his out before him, one in each hand.

The last thing I see before we hit the ground are two sets of blue eyes watching me.

My daughters.

They stare at me, bright blue eyes boring into my soul.

And then the serpent's mouth opens and falls to my neck, and the darkness comes.

CHAPTER 15

VORTEX

The wind has stopped.

I can no longer feel my body, nor hear Tessa. The sounds of fighting have disappeared, sucked into a place I no longer belong to. I can't tell if my eyes are open or closed. I'm lying down, afloat on a square, mist-filled sea, my only companions four strange faces at each outer corner. A spiral of sweet-smelling smoke forms a fragile thread that runs from me to each face. To my right, the face seems to be a butterfly with human eyes. From my left stares an unblinking toad. Before me, in the direction my feet point, are the keen eyes and brilliant colors of a scarlet macaw. Behind, looming menacingly over me, is a sharp-beaked avian face I do not recognize. When it speaks, though, I hear a deep, masculine human voice. It is nothing like Katiusca's light chattering, yet I know it is he that speaks. I understand his words, though I could not say what language we are speaking.

"You are almost empty, child."

I shiver, and the trails of smoke before me shimmer.

"But here, in this moment, you are human still, and the choice remains yours. No man can choose the water path another soul must travel, and so I will ask you: do you choose this path?"

I understand what he means by *water path*. I see them, the different water paths, stretched out before me, gleaming gold and turquoise and indigo, a myriad of colors, each distinct yet oddly intertwined. I know them for what they are: different lives, but all lives I have led, might lead, or could have led. I can see in them past and future, memories and strange visions, and I am poised at their nexus, at a central point where I might choose which of the water paths I follow.

Scenes surround me, blocking out Katiusca, blocking out everything. The spiraling smoke linking me to the four faces weakens further as I fall deeper into the gleaming water paths. I want to speak, but although I can see things before me, I can't articulate them.

I'm barely two. Tessa and I are in the same bed, clinging to one another while somewhere in the distance, our parents argue.

I'm not even three. Tessa and I hold hands beside an open grave. Somebody is speaking: "Say goodbye to your father . . ."

I'm eight, playing hide-and-seek, and hear laughter by the tree. Tessa whispering to someone I can't see: "Quickly! Go. She's here."

Tessa in the hospital at ten, looking at me with frightened eyes: "I don't want to die, Harper . . ."

Connor, lanky and tall, on our doorstep: "Can I come and stay awhile? Dad's gone again . . ."

The memories come and go. Childhood. Teenage years. Gravesides and funerals, boxes and empty houses. It feels gray and exhausting, heavy, and I feel myself drifting away, the smoke threads that hold me to this place growing paler, almost disappearing.

Then I see a tall figure standing by a teal Chevy, eyes the color of a Mississippi storm diving into my soul:

"You're listening to Ludovico Einaudi . . ."

". . . Yes. I Giorni . . ."

The smoke threads shimmer then thicken, becoming more dense around me, the four faces reappearing through the gloom.

I see an old church, smell mahogany and red magnolia, an emerald ring gleaming amid mellow sunlight.

"Will you wear yours?"

". . . Always."

The smoke sharpens, then suddenly clears to reveal the shaman Katiusca, sitting cross-legged, his eyes on me sharp with an intelligence I didn't understand before now.

"Then your choice is made, and we will walk this path together, child."

He doesn't speak aloud, but I understand him nonetheless.

"You will be given the immortal blood," he says, "and then you will die. For a time, what you see will be neither real nor dream. It is both endless, and nothing." There is no pity in his face, nor any need for it.

I'm aware of my mouth opening. A rich, potent force enters it, flowing into me. It seems to fall into an empty void until it hits the very base of my spine, and then it spirals upward, a fierce, molten heat coursing through my body, reaching into every furthest cell and bone marrow, fundamentally altering the substance of my soul and being. The smoke spirals become shimmering ropes that spin out to all four faces, anchors holding me firmly in place.

Suddenly there is a sharp pain; and then it all disappears.

～

I AM FLOATING ABOVE THE PLATFORM.

Below, my lifeless body slumps on the floorboards before Katiusca's cross-legged figure, my neck at an unnatural angle. The final pendant, the vial of my and Antoine's blood, lies at the end of its chain on the floor by my wide, unseeing eyes. Iara is on her knees beside me, her mouth covered with blood, staring at my fallen body with haunted eyes. The three of us are surrounded by a shimmering serpent made of rainbow-hued mist. It encircles the platform in a writhing mass of gold, turquoise, and indigo, creating what looks from the outside like a wall of wavering, brilliant color, behind which all is concealed to any onlooker but me.

Antoine, his face torn by emotion, roars my name in fury as he beats futilely at the wall of shimmering mist. Cass stands with her back to his and her lips bared to show her fangs, beating off two newborn vampires that snap viciously. "Antoine!" Cass screams. "Antoine! Help me!" Beyond her, Connor is snarling as he leaps at the newborns, tearing pieces from them.

I drift overhead. Beyond the fighting figures, Keziah stands by the trees, watching the fight unfold with a red light gleaming in her eyes. As I hover above her, she becomes very still, casting her eyes upward as if she senses me. Tensing, she casts a final look at Antoine and Cass, then turns toward the mansion.

I drift with her. She is running, and I know that she is moving at the lightning speed vampires do, but it doesn't feel that way to me. Time is slowed, the sky and I one and the same, just as Keziah is. I can feel the movement of her body, the strange dark force that propels her. I am with her as she leaps to the window ledge beyond my bedroom. She perches there, and I am beside her as she looks inside.

Callie is in the corner where I left her. Guidry, in wolf form, crouches in front of her protectively, snarling in fury. Before him, a furious battle is taking place. Tate and one newborn are tangled in a fight that I could slow down if I wished, but there is no need, for it is no more than a tangle of teeth and limbs. Jeremiah is whirling in neat, fierce movements, the two swords in his hands sweeping down with deadly accuracy, every stroke of the frankincense blades causing the newborn vampires he is fighting to shriek with pain. Keziah trembles with anger and I feel her tense, readying to spring.

No!

I am formless and cannot speak. But Keziah stops as surely as if I called directly to her and turns her head, growling. Guidry's wolf's head snaps around, topaz eyes gleaming with predatory intent.

I cannot control the form I have. Instead, I focus on the platform at the bottom of the slope, willing myself there—and suddenly there I am, on the opposite side of the pagoda to the river, where Antoine has turned to help Cass fight off the newborns. But I do not float through the wall, back to my body. Instead, I am held amid the rainbow colors, still facing uphill toward the mansion and Keziah. And though she cannot see me, Keziah knows something is there, her red eyes searching the pagoda, casting around the ground that surrounds it. She leaps down from the window, coming to perch on a nearby tree.

"You cannot beat me, shaman," she hisses. "Whatever you are, you will become mine. All you have made will be mine, and I will be whole again." She looks around, searching for me. "Come to me," she commands. "Show yourself."

I hover, unable to change, unable to do anything other than watch her. I can hear Antoine fighting. I want to be there, to help him. I want to be back in the mansion, with Aurelia and Marguerite. But everything I want is substantial, and I am not. I am not really *here* at all.

Keziah hisses again. "Very well. If you will not give me the Abatey, I will take those of her blood."

She turns back to the mansion and leaps from the tree into the air. I want to scream, but I cannot. I want to follow her, but I cannot do that either.

A force behind the rainbow wall is sucking me back onto the platform, and as it does, the first thread of a new day shows on the horizon over the river, a gleam of gold amid the purple storm.

As I disappear behind the rainbow wall and into the space cleared by the serpent, time stops.

Keziah's form halts midair on her way back to the mansion. The trees cease to sway. On the river side of the platform, Antoine no longer fights but is frozen mid-blow, his face caught in an open-mouthed, savage cry of pain and anger.

I am sitting cross-legged on the floor across from Katiusca.

"Now it is time we become one." His mouth does not move but again, I understand him. I wonder that I did not truly see or hear him before this. It is not that his human form is changed, for that is as it ever was. It is that now, when I face him, I see, hear, and feel more than his human form. I see within him, to the force at his essence, something far greater than his simple human flesh. "When this is done," his voice echoes within me, "all that you are now will be no longer, and you will not know yourself. Do you remember what you saw in your bedroom?"

He shows me the image of Callie clutching Aurelia and Marguerite to her chest, bloody knife held out before her, Guidry snarling at Keziah's form approaching the window.

"When time starts again," he says in my mind, "you will not know yourself, but this will still be real. Only you, and you alone, have the power to change the outcome. Whatever you become when you rise from death, something of who you are now will still live within you. It cannot be swept away, no matter how strong the force.

"You chose this water path, but when you are reborn, it will be into a violent ocean in which my voice is but one drop of rain. Only your own inner voice can calm the ocean and find your path. And only you can choose to listen to it. The actions you choose from here will define what you become, and you must choose wisely—for if you do not, your children will be lost forever."

His words swirl about me, there but not, hard to discern from the serpent smoke clouding my mind.

"Nod if you hear me." His voice is suddenly sharp, commanding. "Touch the vial on your neck to show me you understand. Touching the vial will make sure your body remembers, even if your mind does not."

It seems to take every ounce of energy I have, but I nod, and raise my hand to the vial. The contents within it feel oddly cold and dead, but when I touch it, for the briefest moment it seems to warm and glow.

"Good." His voice is still only in my head. Iara, I realize, is no longer here. "She is gone," says Katiusca's voice. "She has joined the fight for your children. If you do not join them soon, the fight will be lost."

Something stirs within me, a vicious, savage feeling I cannot quite name.

I look at Katiusca.

Do it, I think.

With a strength I could not have imagined in his small figure, Katiusca takes me into his arms, laying my body across his crossed legs so I face him, my mouth touching his neck. Over his shoulder, I see the thread of dawn turn to a glow. He touches the tip of his knife to his neck, pressing my open, dead mouth to the small crimson drop that forms there.

It is enough.

As the sun's first rays pierce my skin, Katiusca's knife plunges into the base of my spine.

The pain is white-hot and unlike anything I have ever known. I scream into his neck, craving more of the crimson life force that is bringing me back to life, but I can take only the smallest taste from the mark he has made. One of his hands is splayed over the place where my heart is encased in my body, and the other wields the knife at my back, slowly carving a spiral into my flesh. As the knife moves, the four-headed smoke serpent wends around us in glistening coils, pouring itself into Katiusca's arm, down into his hand, through the blade, and into my body. It brings with it the blazing fire of the sun, spreading it with Katiusca's blood in a radiant, vital force through every cell of my body. Each tug of the blade sears the combined forces of serpent and sun into my body.

The searing pain begins to fade, and with it, Katiusca's strength. He draws back slightly, so I can see into his eyes one last time, into the man he has been, the gift he is giving me. Then the eyes harden, and I hear his voice, deep and commanding.

Now, you drink.

He raises the knife and with one quick, lethal slash, opens his throat.

I sink my mouth into his neck without thought or hesitation, drowning in the nectar that flows from it, drawing it into my broken body, reveling in the liquid potency as it runs into me. As it does, I feel the latent power of Iara's immortal blood come to life within the cells it so recently penetrated.

It is not just Iara I feel, but the spirits who live in her blood.

There is the distant yet vital power of Iara's human parents. Her mother, the hoarotu, is a warm, rich, pulsating presence. She locks my body to the earth below and river beyond, filling me with the power of the trees and grass, of living things—but this is a power I inherently know. It is familiar to me and I welcome it easily.

Iara's wisiratu father feels high and clear, like an eagle analyzing what I feel and see, helping me understand it, guiding the serpent in my body.

I feel both of the shamans within Iara's blood. But only as a secondary shade, rather than a primary color. I feel them as part of Iara herself, her complexity and power.

I feel the bahanarotu, Iara's companion spirit.

He is no longer her enemy, I realize, but her ally, her partner in what she creates with me. It is he who turns the blade in my spine, helping me understand the material itself, the weld of the steel, the way it is made and how it works. He helps to create a flame that closes the spiral in my flesh, then forces the blade to spin out. I catch it in my hand and watch as it bursts into flame at his bidding and becomes no more than ash, falling away to the floor.

The bahanarotu helps me to feel the floorboards under me and know I can bend and warp them with no more than a thought. I can feel everything man has made: the clothes I'm wearing; the nails in the wood. They are mine, and I can make of them whatever I wish.

But by far the most powerful and overwhelming of them all is Katiusca's presence, within me, throughout me.

I feel his extraordinary power in every cell. His ancestral knowledge is mine, as powerful as if I were born with it. I understand all he ever did, ever learned, or ever was, as if I have lived it myself; for I have.

He is me and I am him. An indivisible being.

A new being.

Katiusca's body, drained and limp, falls to the floor, taking his voice with it, for his voice is mine now. Katiusca the shaman has disappeared, but I no longer need him. The serpent he wrought will live inside me forever, as will the shaman he was. I feel that part of me reach eagerly toward the other shamans who live in Iara's blood. They twist and turn as they fight toward the serpent and sun inside me, their individual threads delving deeper, into the very lining of my flesh, where the force of the Abatey lives.

And then I feel it: the moment serpent, shamans, and Abatey meet. I feel it like the shock of galaxies colliding.

I realize I never had any true idea of what it was that lived within my veins, the tidal power of the water goddess, Abatey. It is overwhelming, like a slow-building, liquid tornado, whirling up from the base of my spine, absorbing all else, and becoming strengthened by what it finds. I'm in the vortex of the tornado, the very particles of my being dissolving into the swirling energy, breaking down all I was, refining, reshaping, and remolding it to create what I am destined to be. The energy grows, the core of me tumbling in a blazing, all-encompassing fever of transformation, until it explodes in a blinding burst of light. Then, for an infinite moment, all is still and silent, on a velvet indigo sea.

I open my eyes.

CHAPTER 16

GUABANCEX

My first sensation is of my hair against my skin. It is unbound, falling in gleaming ripples to my waist, and it feels like a cool waterfall. The skin beneath it, *my* skin, glows like crushed pearl, the serpent's mist and golden sun combined. The floorboards feel deliciously cool and rich. I can see every tree from which they were cut. On the still surface of the pond, directly in front of where I am lying, the two lilies that have remained stubbornly closed are beginning to slowly open.

I come to my feet.

My torn, blood-soaked dress lies forgotten on the platform beside Katiusca's body. In my mind, a picture appears of a silk sheath in midnight indigo, the color of the place I was reborn. The bahanarotu twists with the serpent inside me, and the picture I see becomes the dress that covers my body. The shimmering wall still gleams around the platform, the figures beyond it still held in time.

I cross the floor and look down into the pond of my night garden. In the hard light cast by the high dawn sky, my face looks back up at me, and I regard it with detached curiosity.

I am exquisitely beautiful. I know this as an objective truth.

Shimmering light moves in my eyes, indigo and emerald, lit from behind by a fierce bronze glow. My hair has become a deep shade of burnished copper that seems alive with inner fire, and it ripples about me in perfect symmetry.

On an impulse, I bare my teeth and feel an exhilarating sharpness as my fangs elongate. With a savage, visceral stab of triumph, I raise my wrist and use them to pierce the surface.

Two droplets of rich, dark blood form on the pearlescent skin. It is no color I have ever known blood to be. It is the indigo of my dress, of midnight, of infinity. I turn my wrist upside down and the droplets fall to the pond below, landing on the two unfurling buds.

They fly open, and I realize they were never lilies at all, but lotuses, formed of a deep, iridescent blue.

The rainbow wall begins to fade, and time begins to move.

"Harper."

I turn in what feels like slow motion, but the way my hair swings in a curtain tells me it has been lightning fast. Antoine is staring at me warily, one hand outstretched. "Harper," he says again.

"Antoine."

My voice sounds like I am inside a cave, the tone rich and hollow all at once. I stare at him. I wonder that I never saw him clearly, before now, the fiery glow just beneath his skin, the shimmering play of light behind his eyes. His scent of cedar and cypress hits my body in a wave of intoxication that makes me sway slightly. He holds out his hand, and I see the carved stone zemi of Guabancex in his palm.

"Keziah," he says, his voice low and urgent. "Keziah is trying to take our babies, Harper."

My head whips around and I see Keziah moving, as if in slow motion, toward the mansion, toward the open windows of my bedroom, where Callie cradles my babies against her. I see

Iara, mouth open in horror, wading through air in a race to beat Keziah to the window.

I shriek, an unearthly sound of fury that shakes the carved masks of the kanobotuma, causing them to fall from the four corners of the platform. I seize the Guabancex from his hand, and in the same movement I become one with the wind, landing within the very same instant on the ledge of my bedroom window, blocking Keziah just as she would swoop through the open shutters.

I glance over my shoulder, inside.

Callie is huddled in the corner, her face pale and set. She is still holding Guidry's blood-soaked knife in her hand. Jeremiah, Guidry, and Tate are whirling and leaping in front of her, fighting off several snarling, red-eyed newborns. Callie's head whips around as I settle on the windowsill, her eyes widening, then darkening with terror as she sees Keziah behind me.

Antoine, Cass, and Iara crash through another window as I turn to face Keziah. They join the battle against the newborns, who squeal in fear and rage. The newborns redouble their efforts, but they are already weakened by frankincense, and I know they are outmatched. They are not the threat.

I turn back to Keziah, who is staring at me with dark, watchful eyes.

"Come," I say. I laugh, a thrilling, exultant sound, and leap over her, into the air, feeling her follow me. I tumble through nothingness and then rise above the treetops, into the wind currents, feeling the warm air caress my skin just as I can the electrical buildup of clouds gathering over the river below.

It is just Keziah and me now.

I spin to face her midair, but Keziah drops to the ground, staring warily up at me. I float down to stand before her, feeling the soft welcome of morning dew beneath my feet.

"What are you?" she stares at me in fascination.

I hold up the Guabancex, and her eyes flare red.

"This was not made to contain you, was it?" I say. "It was you who created the zemi, and you who used its power to make yourself immortal. You should not have bound yourself to something so fragile, Keziah." I flip the Guabancex into the air and bind it in the breeze so it hovers, gleaming, in the pale, hard predawn light between us. Keziah stares at it then back at me. I feel her intention to flee before she has so much as tensed the first muscle, and when I clasp her arm, I hold her as easily as if she were a featherweight.

"No," I say softly. "This ends now, Keziah. You were exiled because you wanted power that does not belong by right to anyone." The words are mine but they are Katiusca's too, have an intonation and a meaning I know comes from him. "You have sought it, been corrupted by it, and corrupted others with it. I see the blood you have spilled, Keziah. Your seduction of the powerful, your persecution of the weak. You've done all this, and for what?" I pluck the Guabancex from the air and place my mouth so close to her ear I can smell the charred death beneath her skin, feel the dark force that sustains her. "You are dead, Keziah," I murmur against her skin. "You were dead long before this day. But now I will call upon your Maker, and send you back to the force you bent to your own will. You once called upon Guabancex to make you, Keziah—but you have never regained the power to call her again." I step away from her, looking with detached curiosity at the fear gleaming in her eyes. "All these years you have tried in vain to recreate the force of the three shamans that was lost to you when you went your separate ways, after you wrought that one, final piece of magic together. Where did the others go, Keziah? Did they see you for what you truly were, that day?"

"You know nothing." Keziah's voice is a low hiss that nonetheless carries over the sounds of fighting still coming from the open windows of the mansion. Her eyes glow with red, malevolent fire.

"No?" I laugh, triumph thrilling in my blood. "I know that you thought to use Antoine, to corrupt the medicine woman inside him to become your servant. And yet, for love of his sister, for his friend Tate, and for the Natchez people you had persecuted, he found the strength to defy you. The second time you tried, the love he held for me gave him strength once more. Then you planned for Cass to be your vehicle. But she, too, loved and was loved in turn. Connor's sacrifice, and Cass's love for him, was enough to strengthen Noya inside her and defy you once again.

"And after both Cass and Antoine took my blood—that was the end of your toys, Keziah. Once again your ambitions were thwarted, as they have been, century after century."

"You know nothing!" Keziah snarls again. "You know nothing of the centuries I have lived, of the power I have wrought. That I will wield still."

"With what?" I step backward, my mouth curving in contempt. "With this?" Once again, I toss the Guabancex into the air. Keziah makes a vicious sound of anger and fear, and leaps for it. I smile slowly, and as her hand closes around the zemi, she turns to me and her mouth opens in a silent *O* as she realizes her mistake.

Beneath the earth under my feet, the tidal force of the river gathers, while over the water the storm clouds are thick, lightning flashing behind the purple. Thunder shakes the sky, splitting the air in a deafening roar. Keziah looks around wildly as the first gust of wind rips through the trees. I raise my hand and in a gleaming, sinuous stream, I release the four-headed serpent of the Warao from the center of my palm.

"Guabancex will not help you now." I twist my hand and the serpent spirals around Keziah, its four gleaming coils holding her fast. "I am the force from which the Guabancex itself is drawn. I hold the Abatey in my blood by birthright and wield the power of the four-headed serpent by creation. I am the same force that you once thought to manipulate. I am the tide that exiled you, the wind that made you, and the storm that will destroy you. The power of the serpent commands them all, and it works now through me."

I rise into the air, riding the wind currents with timeless ease as I bear Keziah upward with me, into the cloudbank and beyond, where the fierce winds of her Maker await.

"Can you hear her?" I call over the wind into Keziah's ear, feeling her tremble beneath me. "The Guabancex? Can you hear her fury coming for you, Keziah? You, who dared to believe you were greater than the very force that gave you this immortal life?"

The heads of the serpent rise over her face, and Keziah's mouth is slowly dragged open. The wind whips about us, sending the glistening clouds into a purple, acrid-smelling vortex of which we are the center. The serpent heads rear back —and then as one, they dive into Keziah's open mouth.

Her shriek splits the sky. Lightning cracks down around us, striking the pagoda far below and splitting it wide open, leaving it burning furiously. The river surges up the banks, swallowing the jetty, and the trees bend almost to the ground under the onslaught. But in the center of our vortex, the air is suddenly, deathly still—and Keziah is whole, unharmed, hanging in the vortex before me.

Keziah smiles at me.

"You are powerful, it is true." Her voice, silky and soft, nonetheless cuts the air, lethal as a knife. "But I have lived long, child. The magic you wield is ancient. But your body is young, and your mind does not yet have the old man's wisdom. You sent the serpent to take me, but long ago I, too, was once a shaman of the Warao who commanded that force. You have given me a *gift*. Your serpent is part of me now. The power that you own fills me, now, too. And this fragile thing, as you call it"— she holds up the Guabancex—"I hold it, not you. And so I thank you, child. For giving me back the power that is rightfully mine. For being so blinded by your arrogance that you thought mere strength could defeat the knowledge of centuries. Centuries you cannot imagine, of suffering and persecution, of death and rebirth. And I will tell you this."

She takes me suddenly into her embrace, her long limbs finding purchase on the wind currents, her unease of only moments ago quite gone as she winds about me.

"Do not forget," she says, one long finger stroking my cheek, "it was my blood that made Iara. I run in your veins too, little girl. You belong to me as surely as does Iara, or Antoine, or Cass. And you have given us all a gift beyond measure—for the twins you bore will make us invincible. Truly immortal. With them at our side, we will walk not only water paths and sky paths, as our ancestors once did. We will walk between worlds themselves, between time and place, as we choose. We will be a family, one feared by all, in every time throughout time. None will be able to defeat us. Wrongs can be righted, history altered. All that is wrong with the world we can correct. All the decisions that have destroyed the forces that guide us can be reversed. We will restore the earth itself, recreate it as it should always have been—a paradise of natural forces."

Her words slip into my soul, and I suddenly see Keziah as I never have before, as the rich, wise, powerful force she was always meant to be. Her eyes hold mine. They are not a dangerous red, I realize with a surge of love. They are a deep, rich crimson, the color of life. I feel her blood in my own, potent and sure.

"Our ancestors did not exile me because they feared my ambition," she whispers against my skin. "They exiled me because they were men who feared a woman's power. The cast me out because of their own ambitions. And look at the destruction that has resulted. Look at what men have done to this world." I see in the swirling clouds the vague shapes of war, of bombs and gunfire, buildings falling and women shrieking in pain and suffering. "Yes," Keziah murmurs. "And for centuries I have sought only to right that wrong, to regain the peace that was lost all that time ago. And now we can do it, child. You and I—we can do this, together."

Sheet lightning turns the sky into a blazing white screen. A strange shadow of doubt lingers behind my conscious mind, but it is hazy, fading into the mist, and I can no longer remember clearly why I would doubt Keziah's words.

"Will you come with me, child?" she whispers. "Will you be mine?"

I stare at her, seeing the face that has whispered to me in my dreams, the ancient being who has created all of us. Who has made this extraordinary life possible.

"Yes," I say, and then I shriek the word exultantly into the wild storm. "Yes, Keziah. I will come with you."

CHAPTER 17

KNIFE

Keziah reaches out her hand, and I take it.

Together, we leap from the center of the vortex into the raging storm, and we ride it, dancing on the wind as we laugh aloud. Keziah turns blazing eyes to me, and I wonder that I have never until now known her true nature, the depth of her wisdom.

"There is so much I will show you," she says. "So much you have yet to learn."

"Yes."

The serpent coils around our joined hands, spiraling in rapid turns, binding us together in an exhilarating tide of power that trembles through my veins, showing me years past, strange places, and terrible suffering, from the many lives Keziah has lived. I touch her face. "You have suffered."

"I have." Her eyes are sorrowful. "There has been so much suffering. But we will change that. We will take the children away from this place, from all the petty fighting. The children are all that matter now. We must keep them safe, you and I." She strokes my face with the zemi itself, and lighting flickers across the sky, throwing her face into stark relief, a mask of unearthly beauty. I gasp with love.

"We will keep the children safe. Yes."

I can see that now—that only Keziah can truly safeguard my twins from the world of power that threatens them.

"You will go," she says, her hand still bound to mine by the serpent. "You must go alone. The others fear me."

"They do not really know you." I feel the serpent's force surge between us. "They don't understand you."

"No." She smiles sadly. "They cannot. They know nothing of the force you are now, of all you are and can be. In time, they will. But not yet. For now, we must take the twins and leave them. You understand that, don't you?"

"I understand." Of course I do.

"They are your babies. Your miracles. You are their mother." Her words trickle into my skin through the serpent's gleaming coils, a bond far greater than anything that joins her to the others. "Yes," Keziah murmurs. "We share something quite different, you and I. We are not Maker and made. We are joined by a force far beyond something so petty. They cannot understand us. You will rescue your children from them, and then we will go where they cannot find us, until we are strong enough to face them again."

We hang in the sky just above the mansion, the storm all around us; but our own vortex is calm and peaceful in its midst, a quiet place where we ride the currents together. Keziah's beautiful crimson eyes reach into my soul, touching her blood within me so it hums with longing. I ache to make her happy, to make her strong again, as she is meant to be.

"Go, now," she says with her heartbreaking smile. "Go, and bring your twins back to me. We will keep them safe, child. Together."

"Together," I say, and I nod, my heart full of love. "I will go now."

She releases my hand and the serpent's coils slip away, leaving me bereft. I flip backwards and drift down on a slow current, until I am suspended, just beyond the window. I look inside.

The fight is all but done. Newborns lie dead on the floor, already beginning to disappear, as the dawn sun reduces their bodies to ash. Guidry lies next to them, two of his legs at a terrible angle. Tate leans over the fallen wolf, feeding him his blood. Jeremiah is holding Guidry's head. Callie is slumped in the corner, cradling my babies close to her, tears streaming down her face as she croons to them. I can hear Antoine, Cass, and Connor in the middle distance, growling as they take down the last of the attacking newborns.

I perch on the windowsill, and Callie turns to me. "Harper," she breathes, her eyes lighting up. "Then Keziah is gone?"

"Do not fear Keziah." I smile, love filling every part of me. "She will not hurt you again, Callie." I reach out my arms. "My children," I say. "My babies."

"They're so beautiful, Harper." I barely hear Callie's words. I have eyes only for the bundles in her arms as she gets shakily to her feet, the bloody knife still in one hand. She looks at me, something like wonder in her eyes. She is almost at the window. "And you . . . Harper, you look like a—a goddess."

I laugh aloud and something, a brief flare of surprise, flashes in Callie's eyes. She is holding the babies toward me, and they are almost through the window and in my arms. I can see the tops of their heads peeping through the swaddling.

"Stop!"

Callie freezes, looking uncertainly over her shoulder. Iara is standing in the doorway, her almond eyes flashing in anger. "Get back, Callie," she snaps. "Get away from the window." Callie pulls the babies close to her and steps back, looking between Iara and me warily.

"You cannot come inside," Iara says to me. Her face is cold

and closed. "You are no longer alive, Harper, and all the magic that once bound this house is gone. Keziah is not bound by it, and you do not hold it. You are a vampire, and I am your Maker. I forbid you from entering."

I feel the shudder of her command ripple through me and halt on the window ledge.

"Iara!" Callie says. "What is going on?"

"Keziah is not dead," Iara says, still holding my eyes. "I can feel her. She is more powerful than she ever was. And now she has control over Harper, too."

"No!" Callie stares at me in horror. On the floor, Guidry stirs uneasily. One eye cracks open and a slit of topaz eyes me warily.

"Callie," I say, my voice trembling slightly. "Give me my children."

I hear Keziah's voice inside me. *No Maker can bind you. Your magic is too strong, and you are bound to this place by ties no one can rival. They can't keep you out. The children are yours. Go inside and take them.*

I reach one arm out tentatively. It is hard, and it hurts to fight Iara's wishes. I want to go to her, to do whatever will make her happy—but above that is my bond with Keziah, a bond far greater than that of mere Maker. We are bound in time beyond place, by magic far older than that of vampires.

I am half expecting to feel a wall holding me at bay, but there is nothing. I flow through the window, Iara's eyes flaring with shock as I slip inside. Jeremiah rushes to Callie's side, and Tate stands up to face me, his fists balled. "I wish none of you harm," I say. "But the children are mine, and I *will* take them." I move slowly forward.

Suddenly Iara is in front of Callie, her eyes flashing dark gold. She reaches into her pocket and draws something out, holding it in front of her like a shield. It is the small, stone zemi of Abatey. The scent of red magnolias stirs the air, soft and sweet on my skin.

"You cannot take them," she says, her voice low and certain. "I will not allow it."

"*You* will not allow it?" I stare at her, incredulous, and then I laugh out loud. The sound ripples through the air, and they all shrink back, eyeing me with a fear I don't really understand. "You think you can wield that statue with any real power, Iara? It is no more than a plaything worshipped by fools who can't begin to understand the forces they play with. It cannot stop me —nor can you. None of you can." I take another step into the room. "You just don't understand, yet. But you will." I turn again to Callie. "I don't want to hurt you. All I want is my children. And you will give them to me."

"I am your Maker, Harper. And you will not take them." Despite my certainty, Iara's words send a faint shiver down my spine. The scent of red magnolias grows stronger, and I can feel the zemi's eyes upon me, the small stone figure seeming to glow in Iara's hand. I feel a vague unease. "Give them to me," I say to Callie again, more strongly this time.

"No," comes a low voice from the door. "She will not."

I look up to see Antoine staring at me, his face pale and stricken. He moves into the room, coming to stand beside Iara, shielding Callie. Cass moves into the room behind him, taking up a place on Iara's other side. They stare me down. Behind them, I'm aware of Guidry's form stirring uneasily on the floor, too weak yet to rise.

"Antoine." I taste his name on my tongue. The soft scent of magnolias seems to emanate from him, intermingled with the sharp, fresh scent of cedar and cypress. He is alluring, magnetic, and I want him with a hard, visceral urge.

The children.

Keziah's voice whispers in my mind, the serpent that binds us reaching for me. The serpent's gleaming coils push Antoine away, behind a thin veil of mist. All I can see are my children in Callie's arms. Then there is a faint stir from outside, and Keziah herself is there, hovering beyond the window. I turn slowly and her crimson eyes reach into my soul, driving away the scent of magnolias and waking me with a sharp, acrid jolt.

Take them, her voice whispers in my heart. *Take them and come to me.*

I turn back to Callie. "Don't get in my way, Antoine." I step forward, my eyes on the squat figure of Abatey in Iara's hand. I can feel it watching me as if it were alive. It is like an itch, irritating the very air around me, and the closer I come to Callie, the more uncomfortable it gets—until suddenly I can't stand it, and my hand darts out to knock the zemi from Iara's grasp.

My fingers touch the carving and a searing, agonizing pain slices through me.

It is as if a knife tears through the serpent's mist, cutting it away and revealing the truth behind it.

Behind me, Keziah cries out, a sharp sound of fury.

No!

Something—a weak, fading thread of consciousness—catches me like a clinging vine. An odd vision passes through my mind, of Antoine and me lying on sun-warmed grass, the twins nestled between us. His eyes, cobalt and gold, staring at me.

Always.

A sharp pain sears my chest, and I look down to find the vial that hangs on my neck glowing a fierce, deep red. I look up to find Antoine staring at me.

Aurelia and Marguerite.

I mouth the names like a benediction.

"They are ours," Antoine says hoarsely, his hand reaching toward me from across the room. "Our miracles, Harper."

Callie stares at me, tears rolling down her cheeks. "Your babies," she whispers. "You told me to keep them safe, Harper, do you remember?"

From the vial, I feel the force of the Abatey. It reaches out toward the stone zemi, through the tear in the serpent's mist, in an indigo stream. It is the same color of the midnight sea upon which I once, long ago, dreamed I was pregnant. The same dark chaos through which I was once carried by my twins back in time. It is also, I realize, the color of my newborn blood—that brought the two lotuses in the pond to life.

The power in the vial at my neck joins with the zemi in Iara's hand to make a rich, indigo force that pushes through the serpent's mist, linking me to the twins in Callie's arms. It leaps like a current between us, a solid, vital cord invisible to any but myself and my babies. Aurelia and Marguerite cry out, the sound cutting my heart through the center, crippling me with a pain unlike any I've ever known, and I suddenly know what I have to do.

Keziah's presence reaches for me, rich and seductive. *Take them.*

No!

Something rises in me, the last of a voice I used to know, a voice that belonged to the girl I used to be. It erupts from my throat in a feeble cry as I wrench the vial from my neck. "Go!" I throw the vial to Callie, who catches it with the hand that doesn't hold the knife, my newborn babies cradled in each of her elbows. "Take my children, Callie, and go!"

Callie's stricken eyes hold mine. In slow motion, she pulls her arms closer, and as if they know what they must do, Aurelia and Marguerite reach out tiny hands, grasping blindly for the ancient knife in Callie's hand.

Then Guidry is on his feet, his eyes blazing. "Rue Vivienne!" he roars. "*Boucher!* Remember, Callie!"

"Callie!" Jeremiah surges forward, arms outstretched. "No!"

"Go," I whisper, tears rolling down my face as I meet Callie's wide, shocked eyes. "Go, and be safe."

Callie's eyes drop to the knife in her hand. Her knuckles whiten as she grips it hard, looking back at me one last time.

"No!" screams Keziah, but she is too late.

Callie and the two babies are gone, vanished into time, taking the girl who was once Harper Marigny with them.

Keziah calls to me, a wild, unearthly shriek.

But I no longer know who—or what—I am.

I am gone, into the storm.

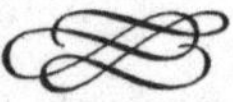

CHAPTER 18

INDIGO

*K*eziah catches me fast enough. Her anger is gone. Whatever held me to the mansion, to Harper's life, is slipping away. I feel only gratitude in her presence, exhilaration in the storm, and excitement at the new world around me.

The storm fades and we travel quickly, riding the wind currents with ease, dancing among the clouds, faster than time. We pass over the Gulf of Mexico, and I inhale the rich, sea-salt smell, feeling it invigorate the cells of my body. Somewhere above the water, Keziah takes my hand, and the serpent winds between us, into my body and back into hers through our joined hands. In the silent way we know each other, she shows me that she understands how the children escaped and does not blame me. I feel gratitude, relief, and a sharp, exhilarating freedom. I am vital and alive, with a companion of my soul, the whole world and eternity laid out before me.

We are in Haiti before the day is high and come to a stop in the city of Port-au-Prince.

"You must feed," Keziah tells me. We're perched on the roof of a white church on a hill. Below us, a shanty town sprawls down the slope, corrugated iron and muddy streets. "Take what you need." Keziah smiles indulgently at me and I feel a surge of love. "There is no need to wait for darkness. The people here know our kind and fear us. They will not dare fight."

She leads me to a roof in a deserted alley, where below us one young man holds a knife to the throat of another, engaged in an argument about money. I realize with a shock that even though they speak in Creole, I have no difficulty understanding what they're saying. In that moment, I know that languages and understanding them is part of the vampiric gift—an awareness of what is being said, rather than the language in which it is spoken.

We land silently in front of them, and the boys break apart, their eyes widening in shock and fear.

Keziah takes one and I the other. My body knows instinctively what to do and I don't hesitate, almost moaning in ecstasy as the boy's blood slips like nectar down my throat. I can feel his ambition and pride, his determination to rise above the poverty of his birth and become something more powerful, as well as the nagging, hidden fear that he may be trapped in the violence and stench here forever.

In the final moment before his life slips from his body, I pull away. Biting into my wrist, I hold it to his mouth, hearing a long-ago voice: *When we take their blood, we take some of that feeling into us, and when we give them ours, those emotions are transmuted . . .*

I hold the boy to my arm, remembering—not the person to whom the voice belongs, for that life is fading from me now— but the lesson itself. I look down as he drinks from me. *You will rise above this place,* I will him, stroking his head with my other hand. *You will become somebody extraordinary.*

"What are you doing?" Keziah knocks the boy from my grasp, sending him tumbling to the dirt. She holds my arm up, the dark droplets drying on my skin. "You must understand," she breathes, her eyes glowing dark red. "You have the Indigo. It is a gift beyond measure. You cannot feed them your blood. It is too precious, too powerful."

Taking my arm, she pulls me back into the air, and we leave the slum behind.

As we fly, she shows me two faces: one man, one woman. The two shamanic companions with whom she was once exiled from the Warao, Darien and Anahita.

Darien was the bahanarotu, Anahita the wisiratu. She, Keziah, had been hoarotu, the one with power over natural forces. After exile, Anahita's ability to summon the serpent was gone. In the new world they ran to, it was now Keziah who had the power, she who could channel the Guabancex.

Keziah shows me the three of them, standing at the mouth of a cave, their arms held over a stone bowl, into which indigo blood the color of my own drips in a steady stream.

We, too, were Indigos. It is a rare, powerful gift, bestowed on perhaps one in a generation—and yet all three of us shared it. Three shamans, all with the Indigo. It is why we knew, even then, that we were special.

I see them in the cave, Keziah using her hoarotu powers to call Guabancex, the power of the storm, in the dark of night. At night, Guabancex is all-powerful and can be used to make them immortal. I see Keziah holding the zemi, the Guabancex whirling about them as they drink one by one, the storm entering them all, binding them as they drink together, sealing immortality into their veins.

Keziah is staring at Darien, her love for him palpable in every cell as she draws in their combined strength with the storm.

We were to live forever, together, he and I.

She holds the Guabancex, using every ounce of her being to anchor the storm's force as Darien wields his knife in Anahita's flesh, making the sun spiral with which I myself am marked. I see Anahita drink once more from the bowl, her beautiful, lean face fierce and triumphant as it rises, still dripping with indigo, and I understand that she needs the blood to seal the sun inside her.

I see Anahita take the knife from Darien and turn it upon him, creating the same sun spiral. She hands him the bowl, watches him through dark, gleaming eyes as he drinks. I feel Keziah's long-ago, human body growing weak with the effort of channeling the Guabancex, hear her calling out to Anahita that she cannot hold the force much longer, begging Anahita to make the mark in her flesh before the sun rises entirely.

Then I see the way Anahita and Darien are staring at each other. I see Anahita's burning, savage eyes as the first rays of sun hit the cave. I hear Keziah's scream of terror as the sun burns her newborn skin, and in it I feel her realization of their terrible, dreadful betrayal.

I see their faces: Anahita's hard triumph, Darien's dark regret. But above all, I feel the devastation of Keziah's heartbreak as she, too, understands—they never intended to give her the sun as they have given it to each other.

Then the sun explodes the bowl in Keziah's hands, and the zemi falls to the floor, taking the Guabancex's power with it.

Keziah is flung back into the cave, and Anahita and Darien are gone.

They had been lovers all along. Anahita had seduced Darien. She needed me only to channel the Guabancex. She always planned to take him from me, to leave me when the magic was done, to condemn me to the darkness.

I feel her sorrow and loneliness at their desertion, the heartache and terror of being alone. I see her in the weeks following their betrayal, hunting animals alone at night, frightened and horrified by her terrible, insatiable thirst for human blood.

Determined not to drink it.

I see the night when loneliness finally gets the better of her, and she approaches a wounded warrior whom she finds by the waterfall one night. But instead of drinking from him as she desperately wants to, she fights the urge and heals his wounds with her potent Indigo blood. Hearing of the miracle, others come to the waterfall, believing the Abatey herself lives there, coming in search of the goddess who healed the warrior.

They brought offerings to the waterfall, worshipped me there as the source of life. I still had the Indigo blood of my birth, even if I was not the Abatey they believed me to be. I had the skills of a hoarotu and Warao powers greater than they knew. I healed their wounds and helped their crops grow. I gave all I had, and in turn they guarded my cave during the day, when I was in danger from the sun. The shamans of their tribe hated my power, though. I told none of them that I drank blood, but the shamans suspected I had a secret. They distrusted me. But by then I was in love and did not care.

I see Macocael standing guard outside the cave, proud to be the one to keep watch over her. I see her gradually fall in love with him, this silent young man who watches over her so patiently. She wishes he would talk, but he cannot.

To Macocael, for the first time, she confides her secret: that she must drink the blood of animals to survive. That she craves the blood of humans, but is horrified by the urge. I see him offer his own wrist to her, the love in his eyes palpable.

I see her drink from him.

Then I knew myself for the first time. I knew my own power, my true power.

I see her eyes change, the gentleness transformed into red flame as she clings to his neck, losing control to the savagery within.

His was no ordinary blood. He was similar to what you are, though his magic was of the earth, not of water. Even still, it was potent, and I almost drained him. I left him barely alive. But his blood changed me, made me something else.

She rises from his fallen body, gleaming with power.

The vision becomes hazy then. Confused. Others, made by Keziah, who also drink from Macocael in order to become immortal; Macocael himself, becoming less human every time he is drunk from. Strengthened by their blood, he is still able to be their sentinel by day, defending their cave and fighting off all attackers—but increasingly animal more than man.

Keziah glosses over these memories, so I catch barely glimpses of the faces.

There was fighting. Her voice in my mind is heavy with sadness. *Some thought we should feed from the Taíno at will, take what we wanted. The Taíno suffered and grew afraid. It hurt me, and Macocael, to see the destruction wrought by those we had made.*

Macocael still loved me. We decided we would leave the others and run, start anew in another place.

On the night we intended to leave, we waited until the others had left to hunt, then made to flee; but we found ourselves surrounded by the shamans of the Taíno.

They have been watching her, she conveys in a series of images. They know the power of Macocael and of the zemi she used to create her kind. They think they need only destroy her, and all the others will fall.

They were wrong, of course. Those I had made ran into the night as soon as they felt the danger, scattering on the wind. They did not come to our rescue. They abandoned their Maker, just as Darien and Anahita had abandoned me.

The shamans use the zemi to bind her. They cut her, draining Keziah of her blood—and then they kill Macocael and force him to drink it.

They thought that they understood how our kind works. They thought that giving him the blood of the demon would make him strong enough to kill me. They understood nothing.

Macocael has already been drained close to death many times, just as he has drunk from vampires over and over. He has not been truly human for a long time. Now, he takes Keziah's blood—so powerful, in such great quantities—and then he seizes upon one of the shamans and drinks from him, becoming immortal. The forces inside him are twisted by the multiple dark forces that are his Makers. Now when he touches the earth, darkness runs through it. Death, rather than life.

He does rise, but he is nothing like Keziah's other progeny. He is dark and powerful, bound to her utterly by bonds of love and loyalty—but half a man, silent and still, master of death.

Terrified of what they have done, the shamans retreat into the cave with the Guabancex zemi. They seal themselves inside as dawn is coming, hoping the two immortals will be killed by the sun.

We were terrified. We knew we could not withstand the sun, and there was no time to find shelter. We ran into the jungle, but it was not enough to shield us from daylight.

Keziah and Macocael burst into flame with the first rays. I feel Keziah's agony, the terrible pain of her death, of losing Macocael all over again.

All through that day I was dead. I remember nothing of that time, only the agony of being burned. I remember nothing—until suddenly I had my body once more, and Macocael stood over me. He had brought me back, as he would a thousand times in the years afterward. I tried to go back to the cave, but I could not find it, nor the Guabancex zemi. The shamans had used their magic to conceal both, and I could no longer wield magic as I once had. We fled together.

Macocael did not need blood to survive, though he drank sometimes, just to keep me company. I died many times before I found the witch who created our talismans. Macocael brought me back, but every time he gave me what ran in his veins, my own blood changed, until one day the Indigo that is my birthright was gone—and I had become this. This . . . dead thing.

We have come to a stop outside the cave, the place where Keziah first became immortal and Macocael what he would be.

She bites her wrist with bitter anger, and blood spills to the ground. It is black and acrid, with the stench of long-dead fire, charred and cold. She stares at me, her eyes haunted.

For centuries now, I have been no more than ash. And after Macocael's death, I could no longer even be reborn as that. But with you at my side, I can be restored. I can become all that I was once more.

Somehow, even after death, still you possess the Abatey. You can save me, remake me. You are not Macocael, dead inside while your body walks still. Your blood is alive and rich, ever replenished. Together, we can walk forever, able to heal those who need it, to wield the power I thought lost long ago.

I can see it: a future where we walk together, her teaching me what I must know, how to channel the tremendous power I hold within.

Yes, she says exultantly. *Yes. We can find Darien, and it will be as it once was—three of us, together once again.*

Darien? I stare at her. *He is still alive?*

A flicker of uncertainty crosses her eyes, a shadow, there and gone again. *I would know if he were not.*

What of Anahita? I ask her silently. *Is she alive still?*

Keziah turns to face me. *I can no longer feel Anahita. But even her power—it is nothing to yours, child. You are the greatest of our kind. You must guard your power well. Feeding others your blood, as you did today, is dangerous. The Indigo is precious, a gift rarely bestowed and highly prized. Do not gift it without thought, for you do not know the power it holds.*

I raise my arm. Holding her eyes, I elongate my fangs and pierce the skin, rich indigo glowing on the pearlescent surface. Silently, I hold it out to her. *Drink, so you can be what you once were, and more.*

Her eyes gleam. She bends over my wrist. Slowly, reverently, as if it were the finest wine, she takes no more than the droplets that lie on the surface; but as if it were a torrent, I see it race through her body, like a light moving through her veins, transforming her. She gasps, holding my face between her hands, and I feel the power flow between us.

She turns me so we stand together before the opening of the cave, and for the first time since we left Deepwater, she speaks aloud. "Come inside," she says, "and our lessons can begin."

Keziah takes my hands, and I follow her into the darkness.

CHAPTER 19

ABATEY

Sleep no longer feels like it did when I was human. The moment I sink into unconsciousness, the voices within me come to life. They are confused, tangled like a ball made of differently colored thread. I cannot discern one from another, nor decide which to heed.

Awake is less complicated.

Keziah is my guide and my companion. Whatever she teaches I learn quickly. Keziah brings the knowledge within me to life, helping me understand how I might wield my power with focus, or use it to influence another. I test my skills in the slums, learning to extract what I need from the minds of others, or to plant things into them.

But when I sleep, it is different.

The voices whisper to me, tugging me down pathways I can't clearly make out. When I try to follow them, a dark mist falls, swallowing all sight and sound. I catch glimpses here and there: a sunlit garden, childish laughter. I wake late one afternoon with the scent of magnolias in my nose—a memory rather than a reality. I can't remember why it was important, but I wake with a bittersweet ache inside.

I emerge to find Keziah gone. It is a rare occurrence. In these early days of my new life, she does not like to leave me alone. She has been taking some of my blood every day—never more than drops, but I know it is not enough to sustain her. Keziah needs blood in far greater quantities than I do; I know she has gone to hunt, and I can't help worrying for her. But after a few moments, I realize it is oddly liberating to find myself alone, though my love for Keziah is such that I feel guilty for even thinking such a thing.

I shift rapidly down to the waterfall. It is a place Keziah tends to avoid, since people do still come there at times to worship, she tells me, and it is safer if we are not seen.

I shift there in a way I know is mine alone. I've learned much about traveling since I turned. I move differently even than Keziah, or others of our kind. I know this not because she taught me—I learned it from one of the hidden, secretive voices inside. Their whispers are elusive and maddeningly obscure, but fascinating, too. Some primal instinct warns me these voices are best kept private, at least for now.

When I'm with Keziah, I travel the winds as she does. It is fast, quicker than any airplane.

Alone, however, like now, I simply dematerialize, the particles of my body disintegrating and reforming at will. I've discovered that so long as I have something to cling to, visualize, or imagine—a scent, a building, the touch of wind or earth on my body— I can transport myself to that place instantaneously. I haven't shared that knowledge with Keziah. I sense she would not like the voices I carry within, nor a skill she does not herself possess.

The waterfall is deserted, the most recent human scent many days cold. I perch on a boulder close to the tumbling water. I feel a strange peace here, in the roaring sound of falling water, the fresh scent of damp greenery. There is something oddly familiar about it, as if I have known the place before.

The rushing curtain of water thins momentarily, and I catch a glimpse of something behind it—a dark opening, like a cave. My interest piqued, I shift through the water. The cave is set back from the waterfall, part of the natural rock formation. It is a low-roofed semicircle, about ten yards wide and deep. It is empty but for a carved stone figure, just over a yard high, which stands over a still pool of clear water. A curious chill touches my skin as I look at it.

It is a woman, squatting with her knees blatantly open, hair like a thick waterfall around her face. Her mouth is wide open. She looks ugly, with her protruding belly, and yet incredibly vital at the same time. I feel a shock of recognition and something else—a tug of memory. I have seen the squat figure before.

A stone figurine falling to the floor. Blood, rich and potent, in a vial at my neck. Two small figures, swaddled and held close by another—

I step closer to the statue, my throat oddly constricted. An opening in the rock roof above sends a shaft of light down onto the stone carving. I reach out to touch it, both fascinated and repelled; but just before I do, the light catches the emerald on my finger, turning it to a brilliant, blinding green fire. I raise my hand, turning it one way and the other, marveling that it is only now I am truly seeing how beautiful it is. Since my transformation I have worn it, but not really seen it.

Take it off.

I don't want to remove the ring. But the whisper seems to come from the stone carving itself, and I have begun to trust these strange messages. I take the emerald off and hold it up to the light. Carved words on the inside catch my eye.

Always. Toujours. Always.

The constriction in my throat tightens. I slip the ring back on my finger, suddenly craving its previously unnoticed weight. In my mind, I see a pair of eyes, deep cobalt shot with gold. Just as when I woke, the air is suddenly rich and sweet with the scent of red magnolias, so thick it is almost like inhaling a drug. The air seems to shimmer the closer I come to the statue, like water stirring on a pond, distorting the lines of the squat figure. A strange breeze stirs the still air of the cave, and it carries a voice that whispers inside me, all around me:

Harper.

I know that voice. I see a pale-faced girl lying in a hospital bed, struggling to sit up, two figures bent over her, trying to calm her. *"Harper!"* she calls, more urgently this time, and her eyes seem to bore into my soul. *"Harper, come back. You have to come back."*

The vision seems to come from the statue, and I think that if I can just reach inside it, I will find my way to the girl on the bed and understand why my chest hurts so much, what it is the voices are trying to say.

With the scent of magnolias, I hear another voice, one that makes my heart tighten and the emerald on my finger glow. *Come back to me, Harper. Please . . .*

Without thought or intention, I reach out to touch the stone statue.

"No!"

Keziah's voice, shrill with fury, cuts through the perfume of magnolias and the whispering voices. She is standing on the other side of the waterfall, and I sense with a sudden, deep certainty that she cannot set foot in the cave.

She cannot follow you.

This voice is deep and sure. It is not one I know, but I trust it instinctively. The statue seems to glow, and I know the voice belongs to the spirit embodied in the stone.

Abatey.

The shaft of light brightens, blazing down on the stone figure so it glows amid the wavering, somnolent air. Outside, Keziah is calling for me to stop, to listen.

But her voice no longer matters.

The statue has given me an odd illumination: all that Keziah has told me, all that she has shown me in her mental pictures, is just a story. Just as one commentator might tell a tale from one perspective, Keziah has given me a story that fits her own narrative. I realize that it is not truth. It is not fact.

With that thought, a jumble of impressions tumble into my mind, voices shouting over one another, so I see the same story from Anahita's perspective, from Darien's.

I hear Keziah's voice, strident and taut: *We can govern all that is known, if you will just do what I say, Darien. Be rulers of all . . .*

I hear Darien, weary, cautious: *We were fighting for natural forces, Keziah. Not for this. Not for such power. It is not natural, not right . . .*

I feel the shifting emotions—Keziah's fear and ambition, her fierce hold upon the other two.

Without needing to be told, I see what really happened.

You are wrong, I think, wonder and compassion twisting inside me. *You do not even see the lie you tell yourself.*

There is so much I want to ask the Abatey before me. What I am now. *Who* I am.

But then I see twin pairs of blue eyes, and the emerald glint upon my finger, and when my mind forms a question, it is a different one, a question I don't even realize I am going to ask until I do.

What do you wish me to do?

I already know the answer, feel it vibrate through me with the certainty of truth.

Go home, the squat figure says to me. *It is time to go home.*

I reach out to the belly of the stone carving, and I touch the Abatey.

～

I AM SUCKED THROUGH SPACE AND TIME WITH DEVASTATING force. This is not the dematerialization I have discovered alone, a gentle dismantling of myself. It is a brutal pulling apart of all that I am, rocketing through nothingness. When I come back to material form, the air about me is sharper, the scents both strange and heartbreakingly familiar. I smell river mud and cypress, lilies and the charred remnants of old fire. The latter comes from a blackened, twisted structure barely feet from where I stand.

I was made there.

The pagoda has fallen in, collapsed atop a garden.

That was my garden.

I look around. Behind me are magnolia trees, but despite the spring air, they are bare of flowers. Their once-vivid petals lie brown and dead on the grass. Sadness hurts my throat. Without thinking, I pierce my thumb with my fangs, so drops of indigo well up, and touch it to a branch.

Immediately, new flowers appear on it, growing and unfurling in barely seconds, filling my senses with the welcome, familiar scent. *Home. This is my home.*

I turn to the mansion above. Lights glow within, and I can hear voices, raised in anger.

I follow the air currents and stay in the shadows, alighting in the live oak beyond the kitchen, hiding in the branches. I can see straight through the open kitchen windows to where a group of people stand, arguing over the top of one another. As I hear each voice, the person's name comes to me, and with it a torrent of recollection.

"We got Cass back. There has to be a way to reach Harper."

Connor.

I know his face. I saw him in the vision I had in the cave. He was sitting by the bedside of the pale-faced girl, the one who called to me.

Tessa.

I hear her name, whispered on the night currents like a sigh. She lives in the earth here, I remember. She was my twin.

Connor is my brother. He is angry; I can see it in his face, feel it in his voice, and I want to comfort him. "We can't just give up on her," he snaps. "We can at least try to find her."

"She's nowhere close by, Connor." A quieter voice, pacifying. *Tate.*

I feel grateful when I think his name, a sense of peace. *He is one of our kind.*

"The wolves haven't caught the faintest scent of Keziah or Harper since they disappeared. Wherever they've gone, it is nowhere we can track them. They aren't feeding anywhere near here, or we'd know."

The next voice is bleak and makes the others fall silent.

"We don't know what Harper has become. You saw her face before she disappeared. The girl you knew is gone. I should know. It happened to me."

Cass.

I stare at her beautiful face, and I remember the night she was made, how she rose from the ground blazing with power.

I shiver. *I was afraid of her then. Are they afraid of me?*

"And like I said, we got you back!" It's Connor again, his voice higher this time, his fear palpable. "Iara, you are her Maker. Surely you must be able to track her—"

"Iara is exhausted." Tate's voice has a sharper edge to it this time, and in the glow of the light, I see the strain on his face as he moves protectively close to a figure who is facing away from me. "She hasn't slept in days. She's barely fed. She's worked every kind of magic she can to try to contact Harper. None of it has worked."

"She's hidden from me." Iara's voice is faint, and I watch her collapse into a chair, Tate holding her arm. She's clearly worn out.

My fault. She's like this because of me.

A sharp stab of guilt pierces my heart. I want to go to her, help her.

You are my Maker. I love you.

The emotion is so strong it pulls me forward, so that despite myself, I'm almost about to materialize in their midst. It takes all my willpower to cling to the tree, stay where I am. Something of what I feel must ripple on the air, because Iara shudders and looks around, eyes narrowing. Nobody else seems to notice, though. They are already arguing amongst themselves again.

"We can't do anything more until Guidry and Antoine return anyway. We should all get some rest. God knows we need it," says Tate, rubbing a hand over his face wearily.

"Really?" This voice is low and furious, almost unfamiliar. A tall figure steps forward. His eyes are dark, sunken pits of rage and hurt.

Jeremiah, I think, but this is not the Jeremiah I remember.

His face is gaunt and much older than his years, and he stares around at the gathering with unmistakable hostility. "Callie is gone." His voice cracks on the last word. "*Gone.* Nobody knows where. Or, rather, *when*—since if Guidry is to be believed, the twins have taken Callie back in time with them, to a place where nobody knows how to reach them.

"And all that any of you are talking about is how to get Harper back. *Harper!*" He shakes his head in frustration. "Harper is a vampire now. And if what Iara says is true, she's not just any old run-of-the-mill kind of vampire. She's some kind of magical creature with powers nobody even understands yet. If she has run off with Keziah, and the two have joined forces, then chances are we won't see her for years—if not centuries. Am I the only one who thinks we're all back to front on this one? Or is it that Callie just doesn't matter to any of you, because she's only a human?" He spits the last word angrily, staring around in accusation. "Callie, Aurelia, and Marguerite have disappeared, too. Shouldn't we be trying to find them instead of the very creatures they were trying to escape?"

A clamor of voices erupts. Tate, trying to pacify Jeremiah. Iara, saying tiredly that without Harper, they have no way of rescuing Callie. Connor shouting that nobody is safe so long as Keziah is out there. But their voices are on the periphery of my consciousness, two words swirling above the noise.

Aurelia and Marguerite.

I see their blue eyes staring at me.

My children.

I grip the tree so hard my hand cuts through it. A branch falls to the earth below. The voices stop abruptly, the faces in the kitchen turning in my direction, every one tense with alarm.

Callie.

She was crying. I told her to go, to save my children.

The very creatures they were trying to escape . . .

Somewhere inside me something breaks with the same finality as the tree branch, ripping me apart.

Jeremiah's words settle inside me like stones, and just like that, the whispers I have heard since the moment I changed become distinct, like different branches of a complex river system.

Like water paths.

I see their different colors, feel their contrasting currents and flow as they thread in and out of each other. In time, I know, I will make sense of each voice.

But at their center is the golden, gleaming current into which they all feed. A water path so wide and deep I wonder I did not see that it was the main river, beyond the confusing estuaries I have been wandering in, lost, since my transformation. Hovering over it is the stone carving in the cave, the figurine that was in Iara's hand. But now the face on that figurine is not the open-mouthed stranger that was the zemi, the Abatey.

It is the face that has looked back at me for the past nineteen years. The face I once shared with my twin sister, Tessa.

It is *my* face.

I shift on the currents just as the figures in the kitchen stir in alarm, and suddenly I am standing in their midst, surrounded by stunned, scared faces.

"I am Harper," I say.

ZEMI

"Don't be afraid."

I can feel their tension, their mingled fascination and horror.

"I won't hurt you, I promise." I look around at the skeptical faces in the room. "But we don't have long. Keziah is on her way. She can't travel as fast as I can, but she knows where I have gone, and she is coming after me." I look outside, where night has fallen completely. "She will be here before the new moon falls behind the river."

"And then what?" Jeremiah's eyes are glittering as he steps forward, shaking off Tate's cautionary arm. "Will you fall back under her spell?"

"No." I meet his gaze steadily. "Keziah is not stronger than me. I simply lost myself for a while, is all. But I'm back now. When she comes, I will fight her, and I will win. But none of you should be here when I do. She will try to use you all to get what she wants."

"And what is that?" Iara asks. Her face is drawn and tired. My heart aches with the efforts I know she has exhausted on my behalf. I kneel before her, looking into the eyes I feel inside myself, the soul that is forever a part of me.

"She wants the twins," I say. "Our children. But she will not have them. Not now, not ever. I will destroy her, so she can never touch any of us again." I cover her hands with my own with a shock of recognition. "Thank you for making me. For holding the Abatey when I could not. You saved my children, and you saved me. For this alone, I love you with all my heart. But I know you, too. Inside myself." Tears rise in my throat. "Your water path is one of the most beautiful within me," I whisper. "It runs beside my own and makes me strong. Thank you, Iara."

Iara's eyes fill. She reaches inside her jacket and pulls out the small stone zemi I touched the last time we met. It is in a leather pouch, hanging on a cord. "You will need this," she says.

I take it, feeling the jolt as it comes into my hand, and put it over my head. It is warm and heavy against my chest. I turn to Jeremiah.

"I will find a way to bring them back," I say. My voice catches in my throat. "I promise, Jeremiah."

He folds his arms and stares at me without answering.

He is tired of our promises, I think. *Of all of this.* I want to touch him, to reassure him, but I know, with a thrill of sadness, that I am no longer something he can trust.

The knowledge hurts.

From the distance comes the sound of wolves calling.

In the next instant I feel a presence, like a thrilling, invisible thread that tightens as it draws near. My body quivers with expectation, rising to a fever pitch. I rematerialize on the back porch.

Antoine is standing before me.

"Harper."

His eyes are liquid cobalt, deep and fathomless, his voice low and rough. He smells of cedar and cypress and the wilds, both within and without, he has traveled in his search for me. Guidry, still in wolf form, prowls silently to stand at his side, watching me through wary topaz eyes.

"Keziah is coming," I say.

He nods slowly, his eyes not leaving my face. "I caught her presence a few moments ago, then the wolves got her scent." His eyes narrow slightly. "Will you go with her?"

"No." I shake my head slightly. "I am myself again. She can no longer control me." I meet his eyes. "But I do have to fight her, Antoine. And it won't be easy. You should leave."

"I will not leave," he says instantly.

"She is stronger since my transformation." I hold his eyes. "She has drunk from me."

Antoine's eyes flare savagely, his hands clenching into fists.

"She will be able to command you. You must leave. All of you. If I am to defeat her, it must be here, on my ground, and it must be alone." The others have emerged from the mansion. "You must take them all to the other side of the river," I say to Antoine. "She will be weakened on wolf ground. Now that she has taken my blood, she will be more dangerous here, where she was once bound and where my blood has strengthened the earth."

"Antoine and I will stay with you. We can resist her." It is Cass, standing tall and strong nearby, her eyes glowing a predatory red. Cass has more than a little of Keziah within her. I can feel the shadow in her blood.

"No." I turn to her. "Not since Keziah has drunk from me. You are not safe here, Cass. Go with the others across the river. I swear to you, I will defeat her."

"You can trust her words." It is Iara who speaks, her voice tired but clear. "Harper knows herself now. We should go. Keziah is coming closer." Her face spasms, and I realize that without the Abatey, Iara is no longer shielded from Keziah's control. I am at her side in an instant. "You must drink from me," I murmur, sinking my fangs into my wrist. "It's the only way you will find the strength to defy her." I hold up my wrist, and Iara's eyes widen when she sees the Indigo glistening on my skin.

"What is it?" Jeremiah asks, his voice both fascinated and repelled as he looks at the twin points on my wrist.

"The Indigo," Iara murmurs, staring at the blood in wonder. "You have the Indigo, Harper."

"What's the Indigo?" Connor asks from behind me, his voice sharp.

"We don't have time for this." I hold my wrist to Iara's mouth. "You must drink, or she will control you, Iara."

Iara nods, and her mouth latches onto my wrist. After a moment, I feel something in her change, her tentative lapping turn to fierce demand, and I wrench away from her mouth. She is crouched before me, her eyes glowing deep purple, and she snarls when I take my arm away.

"Iara." Tate, frowning, puts his hand out. Iara looks at him and back at me, then seems to come out of her trance, her face shocked and confused.

"We need to leave," she says abruptly. She looks around at the others. "Harper is right. There are powers here greater than us all. None of us are safe. Come, now. Quickly." She turns and runs down the slope, Tate behind her. The others follow, all except Antoine and Jeremiah, who is standing on the porch, glaring at me.

"When you defeat Keziah," he says, "do you promise to bring Callie back?"

"Jeremiah!" It's Guidry, in human form, a blanket wrapped around his waist. "That's enough."

"No, Guidry." Jeremiah stares back at the wolf with such hostility it makes me take a step back in surprise. "It's me who's had enough. Of you and your lies. You knew that Callie would go. You even told her *where* to go. And now you won't tell us anything, even though you plainly knew all along what would happen. Don't you dare tell me what is enough. The only reason you're not dead is because Antoine thinks you might actually be able to help. But if it was up to me—believe me—you'd be dead, Guidry."

"Jeremiah." Antoine's face is dark. "This isn't the time—"

"Time?" Jeremiah smiles, a tight, hard thing without any warmth. "Don't talk to me about *time*, Antoine."

I feel a pressure in the air, a darkness coming closer. "We cannot talk about this right now," I say, looking at them. "Go, now. Keziah is coming."

Jeremiah opens his mouth to argue, but Antoine simply picks him up, bundling the tall figure under his arm as if Jeremiah were a toy. Guidry leaps into the air, sending the blanket flying as he transforms mid-leap. Antoine gives me a final look. "I will be waiting," he says grimly.

I meet his eyes. "Always," I say softly.

His eyes flare in surprise, and then he is gone, and I am standing alone on the porch, waiting.

CHAPTER 21

HARPER

I see Keziah coming, aloft on the wind currents, though I doubt anyone else could. What to any other would be no more than a presence, to me is as clear as a motion picture. I feel her anger and tension, sense her fear. When she comes to a halt, wide-legged, in front of me, I know all she feels as if it were my own soul.

You are confused. Her eyes glitter. *You must come with me, before this ground weakens your mind and confuses your thoughts. They bound me here. For centuries, I lay under this earth, in the dark and the cold.* She shows me the pictures in her mind, and I can't suppress a shudder as I feel it—the horrible, slow fading, the despair and terror as thirst turned into agony, then finally into a pale shadow life.

I leap to the ground, feeling the damp, dew-covered grass beneath my bare feet, and it's my turn. I show her the images held in the earth itself: generations of Marigny women, driven mad by Keziah's whispers. Families torn apart by madness, death, and grief. A large, leather-covered bible open, Antoine pointing grimly to the names on it, showing generation after generation their obligation—to keep the demons bound in the cellar below. Ashen-faced Marigny descendants arguing, shouting, trying to understand, reeling from Antoine in horror. The family's gradual fall into madness, despair, and poverty, the mansion eventually abandoned and falling into decay.

I show her Cass, lying bleeding on the floor, red eyes staring from her gaunt face, saying: *"You mean I need to choose whether I live or die?"*

Antoine, when he was under Keziah's control, hard-faced, saying: *"I'm barely holding on, Harper."*

"You did all of that." I say the words aloud, and Keziah flinches.

Because I was angry. They hurt me. Kept me captive.

"Because you tortured them."

I show her the images that live in the earth. Slaves running from her in fear. The fields ablaze as she and Caleb—Macocael, as I know him now to be—striding red-eyed through the carnage, laughing aloud at the destruction.

A Natchez village, the earth running with blood.

A shadow of anger crosses her face. *You do not know the centuries of pain I have lived. The countless hundreds of humans who have tried to capture me, destroy me. I have lived as much of my life the captive of cruelty as I have free.* She begins to show me the images, of times and civilizations long past, and I brush them away impatiently.

"I have seen all of this," I say aloud. "I know what you have suffered, Keziah. But you have always chosen the path of darkness, of danger. In all of those scenes, you are hungry for power. You have searched for Darien and Anahita throughout the ages, doing all you can to regain the power you lost. You do not care for others. Within you there is only the terrible craving for power. Not even, any longer, for what that power can bring. You want only to possess it again. In the end, even your love for Macocael died, shriveled up with whatever magic once lived in his blood."

That is why you must trust me. Why your blood is so precious.

She extends a hand toward me, her eyes wide and luminous.

I am the only one who truly knows what runs in your veins, how to harness the Indigo, save it from waste. If you do not allow me to guide you, your power will be taken just as mine was, used by others to further their own gains. You must let me help you.

"You do not use my name. Why is that?" I step forward, so she is close enough to touch. "You have not said my name since my transformation. You have called me *child,* or *little one.* But you have not called me by my name." Keziah's face spasms then stills, as if she's fighting to keep herself under control. "You do not like me to use yours, either. Shall I tell you why that is, Keziah?"

I taste her name on my tongue as she takes an involuntary step backward, hissing softly.

"When we name something, we give it form." I smile, and she recoils further. "I am *Harper.*"

I pause, wait a moment, and say it again, savoring the syllables slowly.

"I am Harper. That is what I came into this world as. I may have transformed, become something altogether new. But my essence, the water path that is me, is held in my name: *Harper.* I know myself by that name, even if I have become different. And you, Keziah—you are held by your name also. You cannot be anything other than the Keziah who urged her companions to seek power beyond what the Warao would allow. The Keziah who had ambition along with the Indigo in her veins, ambition that drove Darien and Anahita to eventually run from you, to flee the terrible need for power they sensed within you." I step even closer. "When you showed me your visions," I say softly, "those memories were there too, Keziah, even if you wanted to hide them. I can travel those water paths. I can see what you hide. The story you tell yourself, the terrible suffering you have endured—these are all shadow pictures, made from your emotions.

"The truth lies in speech, for no matter what we feel, our words create what *is*. And I can see behind your visions, Keziah, behind the story you tell, to the truth of your words. I know how you manipulated both Darien and Anahita—even if you, after all these years, are so lost in your own story you can no longer remember that. I know the truth of your story, Keziah, and I am no longer captive to it. I do not feel pity for you. For you were never a victim, no matter the lies you tell yourself."

Keziah's eyes glow red with fury, her whole body trembling. "If you know so much of what speech can do, little girl, then you know how dangerous it can be." Keziah draws herself up and holds out her hand, the Guabancex zemi sitting in her palm. "I have your Indigo inside me now, child. It has brought me back to life, as I was all those years ago when I was made immortal by Guabancex. You are powerful, yes. But I told you once before— you do not possess the knowledge I do. You have not lived through all I have."

"Oh, you're wrong." I smile, and the Abatey zemi glows warm against my chest. "You forget that your water path lives within me, showing me all you are, and all you ever have been." The fire in Keziah's eyes wavers, a shadow of fear growing behind it. "I have lived every word you have spoken, every emotion you have felt, and every lesson you have learned. All I need do is travel your water path to know how to destroy you. But I won't have to, Keziah. I already know how this goes. And so do you." The fear turns her eyes black. With lightning speed, Keziah spins, but I am too fast, landing on the other side of her, my hand closing on her arm. "I have told you once before," I say. "You cannot outrun me. You cannot lose me. And you cannot defeat me, Keziah. You know that."

"You will not destroy me," she shouts. "It is against your nature, Abatey. You are born to give life, not take it."

"You think you can name me," I say as she raises the Guabancex, her eyes blazing with fury. "You think that is all I am: *Abatey.* You say that name as if you understand it—but you understand nothing. *Abatey* is part of what I am. But it is not *who* I am." I touch the figurine in its pouch at my chest. The leather falls away, and the zemi glows a deep, rich purple against my bare skin. Keziah stares, fascinated despite herself, turning the Guabancex in her hand. "It is not the Abatey who will end you now," I say softly. "It is Harper Marigny, whose children you thought to steal, and whose friends you killed without thought. Whose husband you almost destroyed."

Keziah raises her eyes to mine. Her mouth curls in a dark smile.

I don't think so.

"Oh," I say aloud, matching her smile with one of my own, "but I do."

I feel the moment she summons it. The wind rises in a sudden, vicious shriek, whipping into the now-familiar vortex. But this time it does not lift me. It does not even touch me. The vortex surrounds only Keziah, the Guabancex binding her in a tornado of her own making, spinning her tall figure as Keziah shrieks her fury against it. I feel the force coming up under the earth, reaching out from the trees around me. It flows through and around me: the pain of the past, of all Keziah has been and all the destruction she has wrought, becoming part of the chaos that created her. The chaos to which she will return.

"The storm that is taking you is far greater than the one you summoned in your making," I say. Keziah is frozen at the center of the tornado, staring at me, my words echoing inside her. "This storm is made of everything that you have been since the day you were reborn with the Guabancex inside you. That zemi you hold is the source of your creation—and now all that you are will return to it.

"But we cannot return to what we were, Keziah. None of us

can. We can only take what we are and accept it, then transform and become stronger. If we can't face our true selves, we weaken, become less, rather than more.

"The story you believe about yourself is not your truth. Your truth is both more powerful and more ugly than you can admit even to yourself. You are no longer the girl who summoned Guabancex back in that cave, the one who made that zemi you hold." I nod at the stone in her hand. "That zemi is a powerful thing, Keziah. But it was built by the person you once were. Not the one you have become.

"Perhaps, if you were prepared to own the truth of what you have been and become, that magic could have been yours again. But you are unable to take responsibility for your choices and their consequences. It is that inability that will destroy you now, forever. The very source of the power you seek has never been held by something beyond you, Keziah. It has always lived within. You're just too blinded by ambition and cowardice to see it.

"Try it, Keziah. Try to wield the magic you think is yours to own."

She opens her mouth in a silent, furious shriek, and the zemi flies up into the air, hovering above the tornado around her. Keziah spins inside the vortex, faster and faster, until her form disappears and becomes part of the storm itself; then the tornado becomes a single stream of silver mist that funnels upward, into the spinning zemi of Guabancex.

The zemi begins to glow, at first a pale violet, then a stronger purple, and then the rich, deep indigo that matches the zemi about my own neck. But it does not stop there. The color deepens, darkening, becoming at first a fathomless black—then seeps in, turning the zemi into a solid black mass upon which the carving becomes indistinct and then, gradually, invisible altogether. The black grows so dense it seems to suck in light from all around it, become so heavy it is like a hole in the atmosphere; then, when it seems it will take the very air with it, the blackness explodes into a thousand coarse fragments.

A dead, charred smell fills the air. The fragments lie on the ground like old coal. I take a deep breath and release it gently over the fragments, which disintegrate further into a coarse, dead powder. I touch the zemi at my neck, turning my hand, and the midnight breeze swirls gently across the ground, carrying with it the rich river scent of wildflowers and greenery, of life and love. It picks up the dirty powder, tumbling the fine grains through the air until they are gone, scattered and absorbed by the scented tide.

I turn my head to the crescent moon, hanging above the water as if it were waiting for the night's outcome. It gleams a hard, bright yellow, its reflection burnished gold on the water.

"I do not know how to travel the water paths to my children," I whisper to it. "Of all the things I know, none of them tell me how to rescue my children and Callie." Tears fill my eyes and tumble down my cheeks, grief seizing my heart. "How am I to find them?" The moon begins to slip behind the water, and I want to hold it, to grasp it close and capture its power of tide and time. "How do I bring them back?"

But the moon does not answer. It simply slides inexorably down, leaving me alone in the night.

As the dark shadows begin to cross the water and move toward me—the figures of my family and friends, those I have hurt and those I have let down—I hear a faint whisper among the leaves.

I am here, Harper, whispers Tessa on a magnolia breeze. *Always, my sister.*

"Stay with me, Tessa," I breathe aloud. "Stay with me—and help me find them."

I draw a deep breath.

"Help me bring them home."

*D*ear Tessa,

It is midnight, and I am writing this sitting on the jetty by the river. The quarter moon hangs over the water. I do not need its light to see these words on the page. Every stroke of ink is as vivid to me as if it were broad day. I can smell the compounds from which the ink itself is made, just as I know the different types of grass growing beneath the surface of the water. If I allow myself to be lost in my new sensory powers, I would be overwhelmed. I can lose myself for long moments simply listening to the breeze around me, to seeds germinating under the earth.

Perhaps that's why I'm writing to you.

These words are a connection between the girl I once was and the being I am now. It's hard to think that it's been only a week since the night I became what I am, the night I lost my children. I haven't even held them, Tessa. My twins don't know who I am. They've never felt my arms around them.

As I wrote those last words, the river water around me stirred with an uneasy current, and storm clouds began to rumble overhead. I have to be careful with my emotions. The water paths within me are volatile, and I am still learning how to work with them. They are not voices, exactly, but rather undercurrents I can be swept into, if I choose. I thought that writing to you might help me stay in the water path that is *Harper*.

I need to focus. Callie and the twins are gone into the past. Unless I can find a way to travel the water paths back to them, none of us are certain they can get home. At least we have some idea where they are. Guidry, it seems, really did have another agenda, just as Tate feared. He had some knowledge of what that night would bring. But even if part of me resents that, I cannot hate him for it. He gave Callie the knife and instructions on where to go. And I don't think even he truly believed it, not until it happened. In his own way, he was trying to keep them safe.

I know all these things not because anyone has spoken to me of them. Some I've heard in snatches of conversation, others in the unspoken words I can sense inside people. I find it difficult now to know what has actually been spoken aloud, and what I simply understand. It isn't so much that I can hear the thoughts of others, but rather that their water paths merge with mine when they are close. In a room, it is difficult for me to remain separate, to not understand at least glimpses of what they think and feel. It is another thing I'm learning.

The only person I can't read this way is Antoine. We have yet to exchange any real conversation or touch. During the brief reunion I had with the others after Keziah's defeat, Antoine said little. He just watched me, his face unreadable. I can't sense his thoughts, but I'm certain he must harbor anger toward me. For deceiving him the night I was made. For being the reason his children are gone. For leaving them.

What kind of mother flees her newborn children?

Thunder cracked overhead just now. My emotions are dangerous, Tessa. I can't give in to them. I have only one purpose now. To find a way to rescue my children and bring Callie back. Jeremiah can barely speak for grief and anger. I can feel the tortured weight of his thoughts even from this distance, the terrible pain he suffers every time he thinks of Callie alone, in a foreign time and place. He is furious at Guidry and just as angry at Antoine. Who in turn blames Guidry, just as Tate does.

I do not have time for such emotions. I need to understand what Guidry knows, then find a way to bring them all home.

And then, Tessa, I will need to leave again.

After all I've done to try to keep them safe, now I must face the truth: that my children will never be safe near me. I can't hide from that truth. If there is one thing I've learned from Keziah's story, it is the importance of accepting responsibility for my choices and their consequences. I made myself into the most powerful being I could conceive. I deceived Antoine in order to do it. And then I was so afraid of what I had become that I did the very thing I had hoped to prevent: I sent our children into danger. And not just our children, but the bravest girl I've ever known, whom I love as my own family. I've sent them all into the unknown past without protection or means for return. And even if, by some miracle, I should find a way to bring them back—what then?

The slightest ripple of my emotions causes water to move and storm clouds to gather. I can no more control the effects of my emotions than I can hold back the tides. How can I allow such a dynamic, wild force anywhere near infants? What will happen if I allow my feelings for Antoine, for example, to explode to the surface? There were times in my human life when the force of us together was so overwhelming it spread into the earth around us. Can you imagine what might happen now that I have become this? I could easily destroy Antoine himself.

I think he knows that, deep down. I suspect it is why he has not tried to speak with me directly, to approach me. I know it is for the best this way. I don't blame him for fearing me. I lied to him. And I am no longer the human girl he fell in love with and married, nor the mother of his children. I am a fierce, wild thing, made of many water paths, some of which I may never be able to control.

We will always be joined by Aurelia and Marguerite, the miracles we created together. I will love them with every particle of my being for the rest of my existence, just as my heart will belong forever to Antoine. But I have no place in their lives.

I do not know what my immortal future holds. When I so much as think of an eternity without Antoine or my children, I'm scared my heartbreak will carve a painful crevasse in the center of the earth. But if I think of my presence bringing yet more pain to all those I love, the crevasse widens and deepens to an unbearable cavern of black shame.

I will find a way to bring our babies home. And then I will leave, and find a way to live this existence I chose. Perhaps, in time, I may learn to live with myself again.

The wolves cleared away the charred remains of the pagoda. Beneath the place where I took Katiusca's life, new blooms have grown. They are irises, a deep, rich indigo color. When I look at them, I cannot help but think it was irises that were the basis for the French fleur-de-lis, symbol of the French monarchy. A symbol drenched in blood and revolution.

My newborn babies are lost somewhere amid that chaos, a teenage girl from two centuries in the future their only protector.

I know you live in the ground here, Tessa. I feel you in every touch of the breeze and petal on the ground. I just hope that when all this is over, and I have brought my children home, that part of you will come with me, too. If I am to wander this earth alone for the rest of eternity, I hope at least that part of you will wander with me.

The moon is sinking behind the water, and I can sense Antoine walking down the slope toward me. I guess we have to talk sometime.

The clouds are gathering, lightning stabbing the earth in the distance.

I am dangerous, Tessa, and nobody is safe.

In my heart, at least, I am and always will be,

Your twin,

Harper

NIGHT SHADE SAMPLE PROLOGUE

PROLOGUE

Dear Tessa,

I just returned from hunting.

I went alone. I'm not yet ready to share that part of myself with Antoine, or anyone else. I'm not sure I even trust myself in those moments when I take human blood. Something happens when I drink that I suspect is beyond what occurs for others. Keziah never said as much, but I saw her looking, sometimes, when I drank. Watching the humans as much as she did me.

Tonight I went inland, away from the river. Through the forest and out onto a small side road. I found a little Mexican bar and grill, a mom-and-pop place with wooden shutters and makeshift tables out front, lanterns hung in the trees. I stayed in the shadows awhile just watching. The people who go there work the land hereabouts for corn or soybeans, on small holdings. I could tell just by looking that the grill is where they come to have a family meal and meet their friends. Children chased one another through the tables, their parents drinking beer from the bottle as they ate the kind of BBQ only Mississippi folks understand. I couldn't look away. It hurt my heart to watch. I thought of you and me when we were small. I thought of the life we used to imagine having, one where we'd get together some place like that and laugh while our own children played with bugs in the dark.

The problem is that as soon as I began thinking those things, the sky clouded over, thunder rumbled, and an uneasy wind scattered the paper plates. It took a moment before I realized the chaos was my fault. And by then, emotion had made me fiercely thirsty.

I took a young man who was on his own. I'd noticed him drinking on the edge of the crowd, a quiet, solemn-faced man, with lonely eyes and a plain face I'm guessing won him few hearts in high school. He looked like he'd long been resigned to a life alone. After everyone fled indoors to escape the storm made by my broken heart, he lingered to clean up, and I took him as he put discarded bottles into a dumpster by the trees.

He tasted like loneliness and introspection, quiet trees and a river in the stillness of dawn. I saw the clapboard house he grew up in and the infirm father he still cares for. I felt the comfort he finds in small things and the part of himself he'd closed off years earlier, the part that might still have dreamed that his life could be more than isolation and sacrifice.

I reached into that part of him as I drank and felt the barriers there fall away. I felt him surrender to me and his pain flow into my own veins. I welcomed it, Tessa. I want the pain. It doesn't hurt me—it seems to travel through me and become something else. I feel the emotions like waste carried along the great water path inside me. Eventually it disappears, transmuted to become just another part of the rich flow in my body, the particles becoming part of an infinite force inside me. I saw a sharp image of the face he sees when he looks in the mirror, lumpy and misshapen far beyond the reality, and felt his relief as the shame and sadness of that image left him. When I put fangs to my own wrist and held the indigo drops to his mouth, I fed him a new image with his own blood. In place of the misshapen face of his imaginings I gave him instead what I saw: a noble, dignified man who is kind and loving, who cares for his father and works the land left to him—not because he has to, but because he takes a quiet pride in it, and joy in the small gifts life gives him. I gave him the idea that somewhere out there is a girl who will see that man for what he is and love him for it.

When he fell away from my wrist, he was changed. Both softer, and yet somehow clearer, his true self beautiful in the plain lines of his face. He looked at me with eyes free of that dark sadness. He won't be alone much longer, I know. I saw his future companion in my mind: a sweet-faced girl from a nearby town, who will come here one night after her truck breaks down. Theirs will be a true meeting of hearts. I couldn't show him that, but I did plant the surety of it in his heart, and I saw the proof when I looked into his eyes.

Part of me understood this about people before I changed: that if only we could see past the fickle surface covering to the beauty within, we could never be cruel or go to war. That if people could understand their own beauty, they would never be unhappy again. Something about my blood helps people truly know themselves, and part of my gift to them is taking the covering away a little, breaking down the barriers that exist within their hearts. This part of what I am is something I love. Something that makes me feel that drinking from them is an exchange, rather than the selfish, predatory act it seemed before I changed.

Yet for all that understanding, I feel only shame and sadness when I look within myself. I can't look in a mirror. I don't want to. I know my surface covering is dramatically beautiful now. That isn't a boast; it's simply the nature of our kind. We are made to be appealing to humans, designed specifically to draw the prey we need to survive. It's strange how when something is so easily gained, it no longer has value. If I'd imagined myself looking this way when I was still human, I'd have been giddy with excitement. Now beauty has no meaning to me at all. My appearance is just my covering. If anyone could see beneath it to the unworthiness within, they would understand, as I do, that I am not deserving even of life—let alone immortality.

I'm writing this sitting atop a tree. I can see my home in the distance. The sun is coming up, and soon I will have to return and confront the mess I left behind. Antoine tried to talk to me last night, but I couldn't face him. I can't look in his eyes, no matter how much I want to. I'm so ashamed, Tessa. I'm devastated and alone and terrified I will never be able to make right what I have done.

I know, deep inside, that there is no way I can travel the water paths to wherever the twins are now. I want to believe otherwise, and I'm certainly going to try. But one of the gifts given by Katiusca's presence inside me is an instinctive knowing of what is and isn't possible for my form. I can transmute much on this plane, in this time. I sense things that have not yet happened, catch glimpses of coming experiences in the blood of those I drink, though this gift is unreliable and sporadic. I can dematerialize at will and recreate my form instantly in another place. My body is perhaps more alive than that of any other vampire. It can still give life to the earth, exchange it with others. My Indigo, as Keziah called it, is not finite, as Caleb's was. I am a renewable resource, to use modern terminology.

The twins have the Indigo; in the moments before I made them leave, I sensed it in their veins. And I carried them in my own body for nine months. I know them, even if I understand what I know now in a way I didn't when I held their bodies in my own. But I can't travel the twisting water paths into the past. I can't cross time. Neither can most humans. Movement across time is a strange, particular gift. It was the twins who had the power to temporarily transport me along those paths with them. But it takes great effort, and I am not certain of how absolute their power is. It is certainly dangerous. I don't want to say it to anyone, but it is possible Callie is lost somewhere along those misty paths, neither here nor there. It is no place for humans to travel. And no place for babies to be navigating.

I don't know how to bring them all back, Tessa. And I can't live with myself until I do.

I was given two miracles, and I lost them both, along with the girl I love as my own heart. I don't see why any divine being would grant me the miracle of their return.

Your twin,
Harper

CHAPTER 1

"Surely you have some kind of plan." Jeremiah's voice, tight with tension, is the first I hear as I come slowly up the steps to the back porch. "We've been talking around in circles for days. We can't just sit here and do nothing."

"I'm honestly not sure what we can do, Jeremiah." Antoine's voice is tired and hoarse. I pause just beyond the entrance. I know I should go inside, be part of the conversation, but I can't seem to make my feet move.

"Maybe you don't know what to do. But Guidry does. Shouldn't we be trying to find him?" Jeremiah's voice is hard with anger.

"I've already told you." Antoine's voice has a tight edge of frustration. "Guidry is gone. He left the moment after he knew Harper was safe and Keziah was dead. If he doesn't want to be found, he won't be. I've known him for centuries. Once in wolf form, he can disguise his scent and slip through any net you might cast. He is gone, and we will not find him. You have to let this go, Jeremiah."

"Let it go?" The frustration and pain in Jeremiah's voice makes me wince. "Guidry met her back then. He knew about this all along. That's why he gave Callie that knife and made her memorize the address in Paris. If he knew she was going to go back, why didn't he stop her? And he must know what happens to her in the past. Why won't he tell us?"

These are questions only I can answer. I'm going to have to face them, before things get even more ugly between the people I love. I brace myself. I've hidden out here long enough.

"Guidry didn't tell you because he can't."

The group of heads swing around to face me. Antoine looks exhausted. It's as if all the centuries he has lived have carved his face like old wood, grim and hard. He stares at me warily, his eyes opaque, masking his thoughts and emotions. His wariness hurts, though I understand it. Tate looks little better, though gaunt and tired. But it's Jeremiah's eyes that hurt the most. Hard and accusing, they stare at me without a trace of their normal understanding.

"Harper." Jeremiah folds his arms in a gesture so reminiscent of Antoine's that it makes my heart twist. "It's about time."

"Even if Guidry wanted to tell you what he knows, he can't." I ignore Jeremiah's hostility; he's got every right to hate me. "I think that's why he left. He can't tell you about the past, because the water paths won't let him. There are some things he can say, others he can't. And I don't believe he knows how to bring Callie back. If he did, he would have found a way to tell us." Antoine, ever practical, is frowning, and I search for the words to explain what I instinctively know. It takes all my self-control to hide my own, tightly held, fury. I might understand what Guidry has done. That doesn't mean I can forgive it. But those emotions are dangerous, likely to result in a tropical storm, or worse. I can't allow myself to feel them. "Guidry waited more than two centuries to be here, at this time," I say carefully. "He's had all that time to try to make sense of whatever facts he has and formulate a plan to help. I don't think even he truly believed it would happen, until now. The water paths back then wouldn't allow him to know what the future held—anymore than they will allow him now to tell you of what occurred in the past." I force myself to meet Jeremiah's eyes. "He lived the past version of these events, but not these ones, not what we do now. If he tries to manipulate them—" I shrug. "I believe he has done all he reasonably can, and that he knows interfering further will possibly endanger us all."

I can't look at Antoine, though I feel his eyes on me like an invisible weight. I know that what I'm saying makes little sense. Antoine's is a mind that takes pleasure in taking apart an engine and reassembling it. What I know cannot be put together in a way he could understand. I can see the twisting pathways in my mind, feel the way they connect and work, but explaining them is like holding mercury. What I know is felt and understood, not unlike breathing was when I was human. I'm aware I'm doing it, but I can't explain the process.

"Water paths," repeats Jeremiah flatly. "What are the water paths? And if there are paths, can't we follow them?"

"Not exactly." I meet Jeremiah's eyes and try not to notice the way he flinches. I remember how it was when Cass first turned, the odd sensation of seeing the girl I'd known blended with someone else and become something entirely new. I know it is the same for Jeremiah— and everyone else—now looking at me. The part of me that is Harper is saddened by that knowledge. Another part of me notices it with detached interest and no emotion at all. "It would be easier if we gathered everyone together and I explained this once, so everyone can understand. Will you call them to come here, so we can talk together?"

"I have to go into town anyway. I'll go and fetch Avery while I'm there." Jeremiah seems only too happy for an excuse to get away.

"I'll fetch Iara and let Connor and Cass know you are back." Tate tries to smile, but it doesn't reach his eyes. I suspect he takes little satisfaction in having been right in his suspicions about Guidry.

A moment later, Antoine and I are alone in the kitchen. Despite the fresh scents of spring outside For , the air between us feels still and heavy. Antoine normally leans against the wall, his long legs crossed. Now, though, he stands in the middle of the room with his legs planted firmly hip-width apart, his arms at his sides, fingers deceptively loose. Every inch of his body screams his tension louder than any words could. He is poised for action, like a lethal animal watching a potential threat and assessing the right course of action. His wariness hurts me as much as the pain in his eyes.

I caused this. I'm the reason for his pain.

"Don't be angry at Guidry." It's all I can think of to say. It's an odd thing that despite my own rage at Guidry's actions, I'm still saddened by the rift between Antoine and his oldest friend.

He makes a harsh sound that is closer to a snarl than anything.

"He just wanted to help."

"By sending our children into the past? A strange way to help."

"We'll find a way to get them back, Antoine. I know we will." I know nothing of the kind, and despite all that has changed, it seems Antoine still knows me well enough to know that, because he doesn't answer—he just watches me. "I will find a way," I go on, my voice faltering slightly. "I don't care what I have to do, Antoine. I promise I will find a way to bring them back to you."

He still doesn't answer. I can't read the expression on his face; despite all the extrasensory gifts I have now, I can't read him any more than I ever could. His water path is hidden from me in a way no other is. I can sense the intensity beneath his skin, but I can't feel the pathways inside him as I can with others. I wonder if he is hiding them from me on purpose. The thought hurts.

"You'll bring them back to *me?*" He repeats the words slowly, emphasizing the last. "And then what, Harper? What happens after we get our children back?" He puts the emphasis on the word *our*. I know what he's asking, but I don't know how to answer him. He takes a small step closer to me. I tense, and he halts. I can see a muscle tightening high on his jaw. "What are you planning, Harper?"

"I can't stay." The words come out reluctantly. I know they need to be said, but knowing it doesn't make the dark pain in his eyes any easier to see. I force myself to meet his gaze. "You know I can't, Antoine."

"Don't tell me what I know." His answer comes hard and fast and hits me with a force that makes me sway where I stand. "You don't have any idea what I know, or what these days have been like." His eyes flash gold on cobalt, the hard gleam I've only ever seen when he's facing an enemy.

Which is how he sees me now, I think sadly. I deserve his anger. I have to face it. I owe him that much, at least.

"You sent our children into the past and ran away with Keziah. Do you think I don't understand both of those decisions?" He stares at me, waiting for answers I know I can't give. "You sent our children back in time to protect them, and you had no control over Keziah's hold on you. Do you think I don't understand what it feels like, to be under her control, doing things other people don't like to protect them? Have we been living the same life these past two years?"

"It isn't the same."

"Of course it's the same." He's suddenly standing right in front of me, his hands splayed on the wall on either side of my head. "Before you faced Keziah, when you and I met in the kitchen, I told you I would be waiting. Do you remember your reply?"

The Indigo surges through me, leaping toward him, a force of nature that is drawn to him, as the inner part of me always has been.

"Always." The word hangs in the air between us, full of magnolias and sunlight and the promises we thought would be forever.

"I still believe that." Antoine's eyes search mine. "Whatever you think you've become now, Harper, whatever monster you believe yourself to be, I know it isn't true. I know who you are inside. No matter how angry Jeremiah is, or how the others might fear you, I know *you*. And I won't let you push me away." He's so close I can breathe him in, every inch of his familiar skin so close I want only to touch it, to lose myself in it.

No.

A moment later, I'm standing on the lawn behind the house, every part of me alert and unbearably aware. Antoine appears on the porch.

"Don't come any closer." He stops, eyeing me cautiously. "I told you I can't stay, Antoine, and I meant it. It's easier if you understand that." The words rasp painfully in my throat. "I'm immortal, stronger than the oldest of our kind. I will always be in existence. It's just a different kind of *Always* than the one we'd imagined. I can't be here, with you. And you can't ask me to stay. It isn't possible." Despite the clear blue sky and bright spring sun, clouds gather over the river behind me, lightning glimmering behind them. Antoine looks to the clouds and back to me, a slight frown creasing his brow, the storm created by my emotion mirrored in his own eyes. "You see?" I tilt my head back toward the turbulent sky. "That is the least of what happens when I allow emotion to rise to the surface. The power inside me . . . You saw what I did to Keziah. The most powerful vampire of our time, and I ended her with little more than a thought. Can you even begin to imagine how much danger my presence will bring to your life—to the lives of our children? Look at the damage I have already done."

The clouds have thickened and darkened as I've spoken, and now thunder rumbles in the distance.

Antoine doesn't flinch. "How is what you are any different from what I was when I was made? How is the danger you pose to me and our children any greater than that I posed to you and Connor? You didn't run then. You wouldn't let me run. And I won't let you do this. Not to our children. Not to me."

His voice breaks on the last words. He looks away over the trees. When he turns back to me, he has regained his composure, though his tension is palpable in his wide-legged stance, the taut muscle in his jaw. "You don't get to make this decision, Harper. Not after everything we've been through to get to here. We will get our children back first, and then we're going to talk about this. If you run, I will follow you—even if I have to run after you forever. No matter where you go, I will hunt you down and bring you back. I know what you're doing, Harper, and I won't let you. I just won't."

The sound of a truck in the driveway cuts through the charged silence. Antoine whirls away from me and stalks inside.

I stay on the lawn until the clouds over the river have dispersed and the thunder is gone.

You have just read a sample of Night Shade, the final book in the Nightgarden Saga. To keep reading, buy on Amazon.

AFTERWORD

If you enjoyed reading the Nightgarden Saga collection, please consider leaving a review on Goodreads or Amazon. Reviews help indie authors more than you can imagine - I can't tell you how much I appreciate them.

You can listen to the music that helped inspire The Nightgarden Saga on Spotify.

Follow me on TikTok: @paulaconstant. Tag me in your review, and I will share and promote you!

You can also join the Nightgarden Readers Facebook group, and chat with others (and me) about the series.

If you would like to be the first to read and review advance copies of upcoming books, please visit www.paulaconstant.com or sign up here.

To buy any of the books in the series, please go to Amazon.

ABOUT THE AUTHOR

Lucy Holden is a pseudonym for Paula Constant, an Australian author who lives in the gorgeous north western pearling town of Broome. She adores gin martinis, dreaming on the beach beneath a full moon, and having pool book club with awesome friends. The name Lucy is taken from the girl who stepped through the wardrobe in the Narnia books, and Holden refers to Paula's beloved first car.

Paula is the author of historical fiction series the Visigoths of Spain, and travel memoirs Slow Journey South and Sahara.

www.paulaconstant.com